2018 First Print Limited 1st Edition
Arch & Gravity with New Lightning Press
In conjunction with
CEC DS

Edited by Boris X

This is a work of fiction

Cover, Design & Proofing
by Taeleen Woodard

Published by Arch & Gravity
PO Box 3804, Centennial CO 80161
Printed in the United States

978-0-692-18427-1
2018957357

Joshua Stelling

Genex of Halcyon

First Edition

Arch & Gravity, Publishers
101

December 29, 2051

Soliloquy

In a city of sapphire, diamond and steel, rain comes from dark heavens. Crystal spires glimmer silver where they touch the heaving sky. Tonight they might be free, in this downpour.

In the wake of a reborn age, storms come from an unsettled sea. The wind gives a low, mourning sigh, between the towers, like loneliness in a duet with peace. The choir rests, the light in their windows showing them dry. There is no thunder from the bridled sky. Spirit manifest, through showers a soloist descends—a young, dark bird on untested wings—through the depths of night and wind.

In the valley Halcyon, a man stands at the intersection of two roads. His arms are out, palms open. His bare chest holds the beat of a tireless, four-chambered heart. It syncopates with the draw of his lungs, tightening muscle over his cascading ribs, anatomy in symphony, driving oxygen. He wears nothing at all, save the rain. Bringing a hand to his head he runs it through his long black hair, water rushing between his fingers. Neurons fire with melody. So he lingers, looking at the sky bearing down on his eyes, drenched in lamplight. Pale skin covers his thick bones. Veins of red and blue run throughout. Naked under the stars' wet eyes, he does not feign anything, as passersby and electric cars slow down.

The chaotic rhythm is on his stolid skin. He may be a fool, bare in the torrent, with his lips parted in a widening smile. Regardless he stands as a monument on this corner. Harmony comes up now behind him.

"Azad. What're you doing?" she says, wrapping his black raincoat onto his shoulders. She ties it quickly above his waist and looks up at him. His smile does not falter, so that she gives one in return. "What the fuck are you doing?" She repeats it softer, tapping his sternum with her fist, though still met only by his grin. "You dumbass. Where'd you leave your clothes?"

At this his laughter breaks open, his eyes shift away, and he shakes his head. He looks at her face again. Her hair is black, her skin fair. She is delicate and strong, confident and young, staring up at him.

His eyes shine pale gray in the dark. Water drips down his long cheeks, as from his black goatee it falls. Azad sweeps his hands up through the rain, through the hard light of cars. His fingertips touch her face. He brings her forward, kissing her forehead.

"What's this?" she asks.

Their unity is poetry; an apparition. In the flash of lights rolling by she smiles at her brother, and he laughs.

Truth is a firefly, this halogen night. Desire itself is in these lights, ignited but for the loss of the sun. Shining clear is the pool of the moon, surrounded in deep clouds. Lost then in the storm, one sapphire drop amid a billion fallen tears—seed of a shy perennial, breaking on the winter road—Harmony looks up at her brother. She is the past meeting the present, waiting for the future. She says,

"Azad, I'm getting cold."

One Moment

"It's an enigma, Harmony," says Orion.

"Is it?" she asks, taking a sea-green pipe from his hand. She puts it to her lips, inhales. A slender coil of white vapor twists from the herbs in the bowl, writhing out of a soft flame. It flowers from her lips toward the ceiling ventilation screen. Water silently flows down the window. The night outside is dimmed, the shaders set halfway to gray. It is dark but for their dim glow, that is warped a little where the water streams. Harmony lives with her brother on the twenty-ninth floor. Reclining with Orion in the gray living room, on a big green couch, watching the powerless, dark 51-inch monitor in the focus of the far wall, she holds the glass absently while pondering his choice of word.

She exhales slowly, smiling. "You're so particular about your words. There's a name for the new pipe."

"Particular," he repeats intently. They pause. He grins.

"He is strange," she says and nods again, slower.

"That's what I said." He quiets, then, "Did he speak?"

Harmony shrugs. "A poem." She smiles. "About flowers, blooming in winter. I guess, just that some do."

Orion smiles as he says, "Flowers for December."

"Yes."

He says, "A paradox."

"You don't think I'm a flower."

"Yes, but you wouldn't believe me. If I said it."

"Of course I would. If you meant it."

He frowns. "Flowers do sometimes bloom in winter."

"Some do. You wouldn't say it."

"I might. I say you're endless. Sexy."

"You're funny."

"My notion is pure," he says. She suppresses another smile. "Meanings are more important than words."

"Maybe."

A quiet passes.

"We were talking about Azad," he says.

"So we were."

"Let him be."

There is a pause while she thinks. She takes a deliberate breath, releases it and says, "I've never understood why. He's my little brother. I guess, what he does is get out of, well, my control."

"You want him to keep his clothes on?"

She touches his arm with the pipe, saying, "No, I don't mean that. But yeah."

He takes it from her, resting it in his hand for a moment in silence. Orion is a solid man, athletic and young. The subtle light of his active mind holds in his eyes. His skin is ashen, his short hair full and brown. A smile curves across his face.

"What?" she asks, returning his grin.

"Nothing. Just . . . that bird has flown."

She rests her head on his shoulder, taking a remote control from beside her feet on the couch. The room is lit in a sulking blue as the monitor comes to life before them, and invisible speakers embedded in the walls begin to sing, gracefully, "Lips curl. Life circles. I might learn in time."

"I like this one," he says.

"Yeppers." She replaces the remote.

"There's such sweet hell in her voice."

They sit quietly, relaxing and listening comfortably. An electric bass rumbles, synthesizers rise, slinking between the crash of percussion. She wails long and passionately. Her voice softens to complete the chorus, "No white dwarf stars. Our brighter fires so quickly expire."

He says, "That's strong."

"It's the opium, Honey."

In answer he restates, "Music is a force of nature."

"Tell me about it," she says. After a thought, she asks, "How so?"

"Well, Poet, rhythm and melody, repetition, lyrical improvisation. It's sex. This journey and destination. Everything is up or it's down. Gravity. Volume. Waves. The moods of your heart." He shrugs his eyebrows, as if to solidify these thoughts in four words, "Life is a song."

Harmony does not reply, but runs her fingers down his chest, over the seams of his pants. Orion grins, kissing the top of her head. She slides intently off the couch, kneels in front of him, and begins to undo his belt. Now Azad appears in the hallway coming from the bedrooms—a large silhouette in the blue. Harmony rises as he enters the room.

"There's the lady-killer now," mutters Orion as he stands, fastening his pants. He beckons with the pipe. "Azad, this is Enigma."

The rain is dissipating when they leave her building. Harmony walks between the two men, holding Orion's hand. All three wear long black raincoats. The city rises to the sky where the streets and sidewalks end, in womanly curves of shining wet gray. Trees, tall and manicured, rise from circles of grass. Electric lights are everywhere, holding back the dark, in windows, on cars rolling quickly by, on rails streaking the sky high above. Winged men fly, shadows racing below the ominous clouds, visible only in moments, flashing through the light between the towers. Angelic wings spread wide they ride the wind in rain, with grace—more than birds and more than men. On the walk the trio moves slowly, watching the night, toward a building in motion, like a shimmering silver octopus, the large tentacled dome of the Public Transport Rail.

People flow through the open, lit chambers. Railcars come on shifting lanes, beneath glowing marquees, seconds apart. Moving steadily, with the organic pulse of the masses, routes adjusting to changing demands, there is not a wait for anyone. The crowd is never still and there are no lines. The apparent chaos is orderly like a clock, every movement precise. There are no tickets, no turnstiles, but six centennial info-bots rise out of the floor. Built of sleek boxes, in the pristine, techno-saturated hub they go often unnoticed, though their green eyes shine. They exist to give information and capably converse about genetics or the weather.

A man passes in the flow of the crowd. Slightly feline, his features are taut, his nose wide. The wild blond of his hair is accented by bright streaks of punk orange. Tall, he moves easily and with grace. Tattoos, visible spikes on his hands and neck, hint at a larger piece beneath. A step to his right are two women. One is a brown-eyed girl, of collar-length lavender hair. At her side is another woman, skinny with dyed red hair, cropped. They wear matching raincoats, crimson with black buttons.

Harmony looks down before meeting his eye. Sayd, where have you been? she wonders.

Digital marquees glow yellow above all the docks. Two bear the word 'Theater', and Harmony is already moving toward one of them. A gray railcar snakes quickly to their dock, across switching lanes, its door slides open and they step inside. As quickly as they are in it and seated it moves.

The hard shapes of the city resolve into a vibrant, water-streaked blur in the railcar's oblong windows. Quiet settles over the passengers, soothed by electric hum, of magnetic propulsion. They fly swiftly, almost silently—above the earth yet beneath the sky. Two silver poles stand at the ellipsoid's foci. A dark man in a long white coat holds on with a lean, long-fingered hand. Two thin arms cross over his abdomen. A small pink boy with red hair watches the man, holding tight to his mother's flat, silver dress.

On a gray cushioned seat is a teen girl, wearing earbuds, presumably pumping music. Her eyes reflect the motion of the windows' light. Her legs are crossed, and her foot moves with an unheard beat. Her hair is shoulder-length, unsubtle waves of blonde, scattered a little. Her eyes are now growing tired, starting to close. Her raincoat is thin, pink and purple, sparkling faintly with an iridescent gleam.

Orion, Harmony and Azad sit across from her. Harmony loosely touches her lover's hand, as a smile plays upon her face, gazing out the window. Orion watches the petite, sneakered foot, tapping at the air before him. Slowly his eyes travel her form, and now meet with hers. She's probably not seventeen, he thinks. Strikingly pretty. The girl smiles at him and then closes her eyes.

He continues to watch her as he feels the train begin to slow, then as it crawls, and when it stops. It is just a moment.

The Theater of Light and Sound

Starlight trickles out of the sky with the falling rain, and the Theater flows as if from those same clouds, like molten steel. It reflects the skyline as abstract glitter; a galaxy in neon. This dark, modern cathedral is jeweled with idols of women and men, winged and posed as guardians or perched demons, angels and incubi. Its many domes shine in the cool light, and its spires arc skyward, built of diamonds, rubber and glass. On the lawn around it are dripping willows and arcing fountains—tributes to a gentle giant, may she not shatter them with her breath. The organic curves of this architectural goddess tonight gleam with a soft rain, which gathers beneath her skirts, tracing away down the gradual slope in dark rivulets.

There is a ring of dancers nearby on the lawn, pulsing with the rhythm of an elemental chant, surrounded by onlookers. These are female acrobats, topless with small, simple loincloths of gold and black skin. A bonfire dances high in their center, crackling with raindrops, persistent tongues lapping at the sky and wildly lighting the girls' painted forms. They swing outward, and coalesce again. Their taut, small-breasted bodies mingle in synchronized, interweaving bends and rising, euphoric prayer.

They chant, turning across the lush blades with bare grass-stained feet.

Angels cross the sky.

"Good evening, Harmony, Azad and Orion," says a cordial centennial as they come to the entrance of the Theater. His head is rain-wet, a silvery case for two bulbous glass-and-steel eyes, friendly though inhuman. One of a dozen black-tied greeters on the lawn he has no legs, his thick torso anchored firmly into the earth. Politely, he greets like friends all who will pass by.

"Good evening," returns Orion.

The metal man says, "Please do enjoy your show," turning his head without another sound, following them with the soft green light of his eyes. As they move on his head turns back to greet the next passersby.

Black marble doors glide open before them.

Just inside the cavernous front room they are met, lady first, by three black coat hooks, on a curved rail overhead. Each has a different voice, though no mouth, and knows them by name, recommending a good show before zipping off with their coats, disappearing through a recess in the wall.

The crowd drinks soda and alcohol, at small black tables. Black chandeliers diffuse the light. The banter is soothed by low music, the techno-noir accented by a large oil painting of ten-dimensional calabi-yau super-strings. Nobody is waiting in line, though elevators populate the walls. Subtle lights give shadows to signs, indicating theaters dedicated to astronomy and pornography, Watts and Nietzsche, one the War Crimes of the 20th Century, and a long string of hallucinatory phrases and names like The Ocean of Odd, Shakespeare, Dangermouse, Leon King and Newton, Julianna, Angel Rey, Dynamic Polymorphism and the Imaginarium. Harmony advances toward an elevator near the middle, indicated as the Theater of Light and Sound. The door opens at their approach.

The elevator lifts them imperceptibly, disorienting in its speed and grace, seeming more like teleportation. The door slides away after just a few seconds, revealing the underside of a large, dimly lit dome.

They are somewhere in the sky. Entering, they look for vacant seats.

From above, a feminine voice softly speaks, "Welcome to the Theater of Light and Sound. We are all destined to be here, tonight. You are and I knew you would be, inevitably. Close your eyes and free your mind for the day. Together we will journey. Free yourself of fear and of superstition. Release your imagination. I will be your guide and entertainer. I am the Theater of Light and Sound."

Harmony closes her eyes, releasing her tension in the comfort of an automatic reclining seat. Through her eyelids she sees the dim lights go out. The Theater speaks. "I am the Theater of Light and Sound. Close your eyes," it repeats. "Know that you have time. Know that it will pass. I will be your guide and entertainer. We are the Theater. We are the Light and Sound. Join with me and release your mind."

Disobediently her thoughts stray. She sees Azad smoking with them before they left tonight. Harmony sighs audibly. She resurrects her smile. I always love these nights, she thinks. Still she sees him. Monolithic in the abstract ocean behind her eyes, frightening for his immaturity, his hair is a gentle storm in the breath of her imagination.

"Know that we are safe."

Anticipating the show, her imagining fades.

"I'm glad that you're here," coos the Theater, dwindling to silence. In the darkness there is nothing, scarcely the sound of the audience breathing.

Slowly comes the sound of an ocean—possibly there all along—exhaling long, breathing out—the tide. A wave heaves and crashes, as a wind blows. A gull calls. "Harmony open your eyes," invites the sky, barely a whisper.

A violin warbles lonely from high. A cello moans. Above there is a dark spiral galaxy, below it one pure gull. She glides, trailing an arc of mist into the stars, expressing the cello's pull in the arrow of her flight. She blurs and divides, as a cell split in three—metallic white, cyan and crimson. Like a trick of depth perception they mirror one another, spreading out. Above, the universe ripples, like a pond with rain. It pulses, in circular waves. The cello breathes. Barely visible, an apparition of a native woman's face looks out, behind the stars. At the iris of this dusty cloud, between her eyes, there is a white hole. The opalescent birds flutter and ascend. As they connect they convulse like opposing dimensions, shattering explosively into shards of color; silver, yellow, green and white, a kaleidoscopic supernova. Cymbals crash. A drum thunders, reverberating from the walls. An electric guitar wails on a large power-chord, over the rhythmic chaos of a newborn symphony.

Like a curtain the imagery falls. A racing landscape rises. Saxophones hover over pounding drums. Steadying, stuttering, they march. A series passes of images both real and animated, at once still and rushed, giving dimension to the music. This music, a full-length modern symphony, comes from all around her. A flute cries. The clear sky runs wet like a watercolor with purple and blue. Light crystallizes, at the end of a held note, cast, like the timeless breath of god through the opening sky. Harmony blinks. The guitar returns, swelling chords as the saxophones roar. Then instantly, with a flicker night has fallen. Gnarled trees stand against moonlight.

Pulling, ashen corpses claw out from the dirt, crumbling, expelled in stop-motion animation from the darkness. They climb upon each other, reaching for the sky, wooden. Their bones stretch long, become limbs, limbs raise up hands spindling into nests and these nests in turn spread out with bone wings. One dove in the hard light sheds a feather to the wind, striking a course for the moon. She glides with a solo of harp strings, expressive with melody. The bass guitar hovers in, on a low purple chord, bulging thickly through the sound, forging a path for primal rhythms.

Deep blue stones sharpen into focus and lengthen skyward, in a druidic ring. On the edges of this primitive circle, saxophones deftly howl. Shadows flicker at unseen flames—wooden corpses dancing. The horns lose their breath, rise, sputter, and go out again. Shadows spread like spilling ink. Time comes and finally fades the drum and sax, with the advent of a clear midnight.

The dome is a window then. Spires rise into the rainy darkness.

A child screams.

The flute weeps in melody, alone. There is silence.

A woman hums a lullaby, and strings rise with her. A light appears in the deep of the black, cold and white. With the next crescendo coming it pulses bright, unfolding three spiral petals. Each petal retracts into a point of light. Her voice is soothing, untouchable. Glimmering outlines of her eyes appear, sweetly and soft as her emotion, now full and pale silver as two moons.

The darkness between them wrinkles intently. Faint crow's feet stretch electric at the corners of her moon-eyes. They blink and the negative space flexes. Her brows become dark wings. Crow's feet turn to feathers. The gull returns, at her third eye, for a second in silhouette. With it comes the natural violin returning, searching quietly, black on black. A cello moans. The edges of the image blur in three faint colors. Her eyes reopen, white like ice, pleading with dark pupils. This lasts but a few seconds, when they close beneath lids of pure night.

The light of reality blooms softly, then grows like day. Harmony whispers, "Rad," as her eyes adjust.

They continue to sit through intermission. Orion asks, "Is metaphor the native language of dreams?" He looks at the dark ceiling, and Harmony follows with her eyes. She does not respond, but allows him time to elaborate. He talks quietly, still high. She can feel him tempted by an epiphany. "The psychic computer makes such strange symphonies." Then it comes, "All language is metaphor, anyway. Somehow, in distorting everything else, sometimes we make clear something that's true."

She reflects just a second, then asks, "So what is it?"

He does not answer, watching the roof which has gone transparent, lit outside, the moon dramatically framed by diamond spires and rain. As they wait for the next show—of three parts—many are filing in and out. The Theater speaks softly from above, "When next you come I will still be here. Take peace for now. The Strange Attractor has informed me that you will all return."

Fall Far

Day rides the magnetic rail. It carries her through the city night, into the featureless darkness of the hills and then back while she sits, listening to her earplug stereo, beating her foot in the air. She watches the people—musicians, mutants, lost children and weirds. There is no destination, no steady loop as the rails themselves shift and change. She is waiting—long enough and fate will surely come to her. She is hungry and tired as the depth of evening comes but entertained by the show—passing in waves that ebb and rise with the hours; a psychedelic raincoat tide.

Three in black raincoats enter her view, and she recognizes fate as the one with blue eyes. He sits across from her again as the door to the station slides shut. Strange I'd see him twice, she thinks. Blows the odds. He was looking at me, like he's looking at me again now—he must be hungry. She smiles and pretends to close her eyes, watching him watch her through her calm eyelashes. A man sings and plays a keyboard, accompanied by a hard bass loop, in her earplugs. "What do you need from me, hey Sexy? I'll give it willingly. Yeah, baby. I want to lay you down. I want to just breathe these dreams inside of you." The hook comes in with a sample and whistling, catchy, and she purses her lips to quietly mime-mumble the melody.

When the railcar stops, this light-eyed, sex-starved stranger stands with his two friends. They exit and Day quickly rises to follow. Taking the plugs from her ears, she drops them into a pocket of her raincoat. "Uh . . . hey!" she stammers, calling louder as they walk away. The three of them turn. He sees her, amid the station, and now she thinks he is familiar.

When she does not speak immediately he asks, "What's up?"

"Not sure." Squinting at him, dark against neon, she says, "I think I've seen you before. Totally. I know. Your name is . . ."

"Orion," he says when she pauses. He grins despite himself, "You a fan of the TLA?"

"Oh," she says. "Nah. Not really."

Smile flattening, he asks, "Ok, what's up then?"

"But I've seen you on TV. You're freakin' good at it."

"Well. I try, anyway."

"I'm Day," she introduces herself, extending her hand. He laughs, and she smiles. "That's my name," she insists, not sure why he laughed.

"I believe you." He takes her hand, but for just a second.

"Odd we'd be on the same train twice, you notice? Then I thought, hey maybe I know him. Anyway. You guys going for dinner? I'm rather hungry. Haven't eaten in two days. But I hate the publics. You Manas?"

He nods, just slightly.

"You know I'm thinking of getting into sports photography." She is smiling. "I'd love to pick your brain." Her pink tongue touches her upper lip, scanning their eyes, holding on Harmony. "Obs you're going home, yes? Don't want to intrude."

Standing in Harmony's living room, with a slow shrug Day removes her raincoat. She stretches, reaching up, shaking out her two small, slender, white-feathered wings.

"You're genex," says Orion, surprised.

"Yep," Day smiles in reply.

"By birth?" he asks.

Harmony says, "I've got some noodles if that'll do?"

"Mmhm," Day replies. "Noodles would be great. Wonderful." Harmony steps into the kitchen, Orion and Azad sit on the couch, and Day crosses her legs beneath her, facing them on the floor. She takes an orange band from the pocket of her plain shorts and pulls her hair behind her head, locking it into a loose ponytail. Orion is watching her. She smiles shyly and diverts her eyes to the walls. Then, looking their way again, "What's your name, quiet one?" she asks, addressing Azad directly for the first time. He gives no sign, if he hears.

Orion answers, "Sometimes the big guy checks out."

"Huh," she says. "I'm born genex, by the way, yes."

"Wish I could fly," Orion says.

"I love flying," she answers, stretching her wings. They reach out nearly to her wrists as she puts out her arms, the soft feathers flexing naturally with her breath.

"Yeah?" he asks.

"Well, not solo. Not yet but I will. I'm very streamlined. I bet you could pick me up with just one arm. I don't weigh much more than a hundo. I know I look like it should be twenty more. I had a mentor back in Vegas who would take me up."

He asks, not moving but to smile, "So you're American?"

She hesitates, folding her wings behind her. After a second she laughs and asks, "Are you aware that you're staring?" She looks down. He is silent but looks away. "That was over a year ago."

"I meet a lot of people," he says, grinning helplessly. He adds, looking at her again, "but you are way prettier than most. What is your ethnicity exactly?"

Harmony returns with noodles and bowls, and a pitcher of water, settling them on the table before seating herself on the couch beside Orion. "Oh, Azad we need glasses! Would you?" He goes. "Well here's dinner anyway," she says.

Day says, "I like your place." Harmony smiles and looks out the window.

She asks, "Where in America are you from?" When Day gives no answer, chewing, "Is your family in town?"

"I was coming here. Chasing my destiny." Day smiles, shrugs and adds, "Ha, mostly I'm German. And Irish, but my great grandma was from Mumbai. You're native?"

Harmony answers simply, feeling herself disarmed somehow, "Kind of. Azad and I were actually born in Brazil, and our dad's Greek. Mom's a lesbian gypsy. At least that's what she calls herself. It's her excuse to never stick around. My dad lives nearby."

"A lesbian gypsy?" Day asks, smiling.

"Yes."

"That sounds pretty."

"Not really."

"Good noodles," she says, laying a half-finished bowl on the floor beside her. "Thank you."

"The weather is going to be beautiful tomorrow," says Orion, reaching over Harmony for the pipe.

"Crafty, Scientist," she whispers, picking it up and handing it to him. "It was beautiful today."

"It rained all day, Poet," he replies, exhaling a puff of thin smoke and handing the slim glass to Harmony.

After putting it to her lips, pulling the vapor into her lungs, she then motions to Day, who nods, reaching out.

Harmony says, "Sometimes I like to get high. Sometimes I like to come down. It's like a day after rain, when a lifted fog leaves the air more than clear. You know?"

Orion responds, playful in half sarcasm, "You are amazing grace."

Day asks, "Sunshine all day tomorrow, right?"

"Hold on. I shall speak with the prophets." Orion taps a button on his large black watch. The display flashes. "Tomorrow night it rains. There's a chance of snow on New Year's Eve."

"I get tired of rain," says Day, clasping her hands together and stretching her bare arms above her head, white shirt rising at her hips. She leans back on the floor, and after a moment of staring at the ceiling, the bared button of her stomach moving with breath, she continues, "I miss the sun. I'm turning so god damn motherfucking pale." Examining the skin of her arm, "I was in Vegas last year, saving my granddad. I spent something like a solid month buck fuck naked on the beach, just tanning. You should've seen me then." For a second she is lost in thought, and the others give no response. Then she says, "May I have a pillow? Thanks for letting me stay the night, by the way."

"Certainly," says Harmony, standing, extending her hand to Orion's shoulder for balance. She walks to the hallway closet. "Modern courtesy, anyway. The couch folds out."

"I'm fine on the floor. It's good for my back. You asked where I'm from . . . well I've been in a lot of places, you know. The cities are all just the same, all around the world now. Grandpa used to say, 'People make a home'

. . . and you all are pretty cool." She talks quietly, as if to herself, "If you knew some of the shitholes I've seen . . . well maybe you have too." She whispers, "There are too few angels in paradise."

"What was that?" asks Harmony, reaching for the pillow on the top shelf. "I'm no angel. Count my wings."

Day wriggles on the floor, feathers poking away from her sides. "Eh, nah. Everyone likes the easy lines. Grandpa used to call me a butterfly. He was far less obnoxious than the toy-boys anyway. Sometimes he called me bumblebee." She laughs. "That was before our disagreement." After a second she adds, "Rich old fool. He wasn't totally senile."

"Where do you live?"

She pauses before saying, with a smile, "I'll tell you more about me tomorrow, if you'd like."

"Then what did you fight about?"

Day says, straight, "I got tired of cleaning up his blood."

Harmony pauses. "He was sick?"

Eventually Day answers, "No. Yes. Really it's a story. I promise you'll hear it. May I get that pillow?"

After a moment's reflection Harmony hands it to her.

"Thank you, Harmony," Day says, sincerely.

What passes between their eyes—Day now reflecting heavy blue like a darkening cloud, Harmony a shock of deep green—is a quiet bit of grace, a portent of what they both do not know.

The Shape of the Hourglass

Chill trance techno plays, low. Fractal designs move in slow psychedelics on his wall; green warms to purple, pink solidifies into gold; in circles of lightning chaos dances. Sayd's deep eyes now close, his thoughts in the past.

I can see her dark eyes, he thinks.

He shakes his head, slowly.

On a recliner, upright at the end of his couch, sits a slim, fair-skinned woman. Her soft brown hair matches her eyes. She stares right through the far wall. The subtle shape of her lips trembles but they do not part, as she sits long in his apartment, holding a glass of good wine.

Her visit brings a storm of memories he had thought long in the past, of starlight and Harmony, Orion and betrayal. The past moves through him, as a momentary refuge, holding his focus away from this moment.

The memory he falls into is her eyes. Like Harmony's they are dark, more sad than afraid, and they see him clearly. Black hair shades her young face, pale, flushed with exertion.

Sayd breathes, but much in his past is unsafe.

Her eyes reflect a sunray, pouring through a wood-framed window. Harmony smiles, missing two teeth in front. She giggles, and he says, You laugh like a squirrel! Frowning, her pale face pinks. Playful, with a hard slug to her arm he runs past.

Years unfurl.

Her black hair tosses, tickling his lithe chest, and Harmony whispers,

We fall in love.

Sayd opens his eyes.

He runs a tattooed hand through his orange hair.

Restless, tired in fractal twilight, soothing the flame of his soul, he feels torn open as he looks up at Faith's sad face.

He wonders, What the hell are we going to do?

Orion will find a way.

Faith has a reason.

This moment stretches long, turning back from a dark horizon. He sits quietly on his couch, in the moonlit glow of her damning prophecy. Rain brushes the window in silence.

Now the memories will not abate.

It is Harmony's verdant eyes, and it is not just the color that shines. It is the penetration, intelligence and her flower of spirit, manifest in that dark teardrop shape—the substance of her glance. A reflection, drawn with the curtain of her lids, strikes him from across the room. My brother. There is the back of Orion's head, the movements of his body.

Simultaneously Sayd remembers the moon as a dim light above the clouds. A light wind caught the ends of dirty gray locks. Sayd retreated a step, knowing his backup would be there soon. He had a big gun, but his badge was too small a shield for his beating heart. The old man sniffled in the moonlight. The scientist was crying, oracle, a devil in shadow. He forced an impish grin, moisture shining on cracked lips.

Late in the evening, as he waits awake, a statue, Faith is quiet company. Her mouth opens, but she holds back, giving no solace or answer. In a low voice she comments only on the weather,

"The wind changes."

Silent Sky

Azad stands, shirtless at his window. Skin painted in moving shadows by the outside light, he watches cars going by below. People are few and far. Watching the rail's hot lamp flash between the towers, gone and back, out of sight and back again, he waits as the windows darken, each in their own time, in apartments across the way. Gray eyes reflect clearly in the glass, watching him. He hears Harmony being fucked by Orion past the wall. Day snores down the hall, faintly. He listens to the electricity, alive in the walls. He hears his very breathing—slowly his ribs rise, rhythmic—and he listens to his thoughts, rivers dancing, into and out of his mind—like the rail with its red lights.

Azad turns from the window. Wandering out into the hall, he stands, watching Day, asleep on the living room floor. Slowly she breathes, in this light golden to toe, partially cocooned in her white wings. Her bare legs are folded to her chest, with her arms held between for warmth. The autoduster rolls quietly past his feet, and he watches the short gray hemisphere as it continues its night's patrol. It peruses the outline of Day, nearly brushing her nose, tickling her feet, but it does not disturb her, and he watches until it disappears into the kitchen. Harmony whimpers louder, in her room down the hall behind him, but Azad just looks at Day. She is like many of the next generation, he thinks. She is aimless though in constant motion, pretty, yet somehow lonesome. Perhaps that is not she but I, he thinks.

Maybe we are not alone. What is a body without direction? What is a soul without ambition? She is cold, so he takes the blanket from his bed and brings it there, laying it over her small form. She does not move, save a flicker of an eyelash.

He doubts her sincerity, but her sexuality and self-awareness are less subtle than thunder, or purple skies.

Azad sits on the couch above her straight into the early morning hours, listening to her breathe—slowly relaxing—and eventually he falls asleep upright, with the present white sounds of the night: buzzes, flickers, Harmony's whispers, laughter, something like birds flirting—always this angelic, soft but electric, fluttering breath.

Near three he wakes for a minute with dreams of wingless flight.

On the floor, on her side in the dark, Day whimpers, quietly, her eyes closed. The blanket wraps her partly. Azad smiles and watches her shoulder, collar, her breathing rhythm. Her eyes move beneath their lids.

December 30

Without Sadness

A few clouds lace the sky at the turn of day. They hang, threadbare and pink in the radiant yellow, gold-brushed sky. Sol, the native star is risen, this pregnant orb of coronal haze, hovering at the horizon, invisible to most in its early hour; a wave of color cresting steel walls.

At this clear sunrise the Strange Attractor powers down lamps throughout the city. The generators rest but the people still endlessly pulse—blood in the asphalt chambers of metropolis' clockwork heart—in cars, or pedestrians on bicycles. Gliding even on the winds above the rails, under the infinite cold of this utopian sky, man is a flurry of motion.

Azad opens his eyes to the summoning light at the living room window. He wipes the spit from his chin, the hair from his face and sits up slowly, yawning. Day is on the floor by his feet. The blanket has been tossed aside. Her hands clasp together over her chest, her shorts pulled low on her hips. Her breath is deep, slow. Azad gets to his feet, and stepping over her he walks to the window, drawn to the shimmering morning light. There he stays, silent, full for forty minutes. Then Day speaks.

"Morning," she says, and he looks to see her standing by him, her thick blonde hair unkempt around her face. "Your name is Azad?" He does not answer. He looks in her large blue eyes and she smiles. Her voice is fuzzy with morning. "That blanket is very warm, quiet one," she says, bending to pick it up from the floor, folding it into a sloppy square in her arms. His eyes return to the window. "What are you doing?" she asks and pauses. "Why don't you talk? Are you afraid of me?" Azad laughs easily, without malice.

"My name is Azad."

"Oh." The gravity of his voice leaves her quiet, if just for a second. "Do you have eggs? I'm very hungry."

"Wait," he says.

He is silent for a long minute and she follows his eyes. The sun is shining. Halcyon moves, as if breathing. "Ok then. What are we waiting for?" she asks.

Still he is quiet, standing at the large glass, rapt in the cityscape. Day puts his blanket on the couch and walks into the kitchen.

It is a small room, white, with a circular glass-top table and four slim white chairs. Romanesque accents and a marble backsplash decorate the cooking space. A television is embedded in the wall. An autogarden, potted in the windowsill, is ripe with red strawberries and a yellow applestalk. Day finds powdered eggs in the refrigerator, taps them into a bowl, blasts them in the microwave oven and sits down with a glass of apple juice.

She looks at the blank screen for a second, then says "Turn on the TV," in a commanding tone. Nothing happens. Near the middle of the table she sees a remote. Releasing a frustrated sigh, she takes it in her hand and clicks on the television.

Azad quietly enters.

"Thank you," she offers through a wet mouthful of eggs. He jellies some toast and sits to her right.

She rolls through the channels, bright with cartoons, boring gray talk shows, past more cartoons, then stops at a movie, to take a bite of her eggs. The camera pans over a forest of burning trees, with a rhythmic violin. It follows into a foxhole, where two men are kneeling in the dirt. They are playing cards. One is dressed as a politician or businessman, in a mud-stained gray suit. The other is a weathered, collared priest. An explosion shakes the earth. "Go fish!" yells the priest, wide-eyed, over the strings. He creeps up to look through the barrier. "We're almost free," he calls back. "Time is running out." His partner exchanges a card with the pile. "Got any queens?" asks the priest, kneeling back to the deck.

"Two." his companion mutters. "No. But so then you must have one." The businessman says, under a rumbling noise of war, "I mean to say, go out fishing."

For a full couple of minutes, Azad watches the yellow apple on the sill, though to the casual eye it is doing nothing of interest. Then he cleans off his plate and leaves Day alone with the show. She giggles as he walks out the door. Looking back, Azad smiles at the lightning-winged young girl in his kitchen.

"Her wings aren't even fully grown," Orion says.

Harmony dresses as he lay out on her bed. Her thick black hair dangles, wet and uncombed, trickling over her bare collar. She is a little too thin, very white, and she might appear fragile, though only to those who have not tested her. Orion knows her every curve, yet the angles of her naked form never tire him.

Her muscles tighten in faultless skin as she pulls a striped sock over one foot, and now looks again to him, saying, her voice softer than the words, "You're jealous, kid. The little slut wants to impress you. She seems so lost . . . no, like somebody lost her. You know it has been quite a while since we had anybody over." She smiles uncertainly.

"You don't like her though?"

"No," says Harmony, frowning, mocking.

He says. "Don't be jealous just cause she's genex, baby. You're my queen. She's lucky to even be in the same room."

"You're cute," she retorts in sarcasm. She throws a sneaker his way and misses, wide. Bouncing off the bed it thuds against the wall, falling to the gray carpet floor. She stares him down, calm.

"Ok," he says with a frustrated smile.

In exasperation she concedes, "Well, maybe I am. Really she is though. Yes I like her fine." She laughs. "Is that what you think I should say? I do kind of wonder where she came from."

He shrugs. "We'd be damned to turn her away."

Harmony looks off, pensive. "I wonder how long she'll stay."

He watches her. "You'd let her?"

"I don't know," she responds, too seriously, taking a modest, blank green t-shirt from on the chair, where other clothes are piled. "Yeah, I guess. How old do you think she is, anyway?"

"I'd say it's hard to guess."

"It's strange," she says, tucking and then untucking her shirt, and buttoning her tight charcoal jeans. Now she crawls onto the bed and kneels next to him.

"True." Then he questions, "Wait, what is?"

"I'm motherfucking jealous. I wish I had wings, you ass."

"Get some," he says, unfazed. "You could be genex."

"She can't even fly."

"When they grow out she will. For real. So could we."

"But does it matter?" Surprisingly upset, she gestures at the off-white walls. "Where would we go?"

"You're not being easy."

"And you never were any good at this. At coping, emotionally." He winces. She says, "I'm sorry."

"What's wrong?"

"I don't know. I just want a wish, Love. I'm sorry." She smiles but looks away from his eyes.

"I'll grant it. Anything. Don't apologize."

"No. I'm alright," she says. "Really damn perfect. I'll probably just see you there."

He leans in and they kiss. Before their lips come apart, she finds her mind in the past.

Guilt comes up from the tightening of her stomach to the tip of her tongue, and she pushes Orion away before he might feel it. In his eyes, for a second she sees his brother's wild, sunlit heart. "I love you," she says, meaning it in full, yet still feeling a need to prove something with the words. Steadily getting away off the bed, she walks out of the room.

The Eye of Orion

There is an answer for him even in her storming eyes. Not the waters of Bali or the bridges of Paris—nothing compares with Harmony. She is there when he wakes. Her form is the goal of evolution, realized, her vulnerable soul, in those green eyes, the jewel of every war, every struggle men have endured in thousands of years. Orion smiles. He writes poetry about her. Her longings pull at his will. In some sense he feels her even now right as she goes, mourning her very discontent.

They were young before gene extension—born in the same year but far apart.

Orion spent his childhood in military academy and Young Galileo camps. Though he studied philosophy and the stars with all of the passion of the most curious, his two sisters were the real wizards of math and hard science. Born to raise their eyes to the stars, Amber and Faith were Orion's first love, his protectors and tutors. Long before he was old enough to understand the promiscuity of his father, or the abandonment of his mother, his two half-sisters held his hand while he opened his eyes to the earth.

Orion was a young man, changes roiling in the world, as humanity cracked open the sky. Astronauts and robots explored Mars, Europa and Io, and launched probes deep into the distance of space. The escape for humanity was mental, bold if mostly fantasy, but to Orion for years then it was encompassing. Meanwhile the oceans of Earth heaved. Global storms came, and waves took millions of lives away. War, he would learn, was itself a storm. Nuclear clouds met the red morning skies. Yet even so there was no apocalypse. Simultaneously the vault of knowledge was opening, genetics and robotics maturing into world-shattering sciences. Hundreds of millions did die in the disasters of the century, yet billions thrived, and the population curve of humanity swept upward. Somewhere just beyond these breaking horizons, the Strange Attractors were being perfected, like a dawning light.

Amber went to study in Spain, post-graduate, early in 2040. Faith, so often at her side, was there visiting on the day she disappeared.

The two sisters were eating together, the last time he would see her, reading, on a bench in April's overcast light, on the lawn of their campus library. Orion was not there, but he saw it later, on his phone, through a camera in a flying drone.

When Faith came home she spoke little for months, withdrawn. Orion could get few answers from her about their sister. Amber simply vanished without a word. She left, before the tech of the Renaissance, and nobody could find her. Weeks passed. Orion's two sisters had long been his catalyst, guiding his ambition. In this she became his martyr.

So despite his impatience, he dedicated his time and energy to learning, as she would have done. Little did he recognize his scale in time, his utter futility, until despite his efforts, complete and without him, like a phoenix from the ashes of an epoch, the Strange Attractors rose up, blinding and new like the sun.

Like a mythic crystal the first SA Systems, created in the labs of the United Nations, granted foresight, calculating the future. This proved to be nearly absolute power, greater than hydrogen bombs, the final solution, truly the end of war. A New Renaissance broke, as an epic wave of light, and overran Orion's dreams.

When Faith was accepted for the valley Halcyon, in Asturias, taking a position as an Iris Interpreter, Orion moved with her. They stayed with his half-brother Sayd.

So his first glimpse of Harmony—her rain-drenched black hair, beneath a black hood over her luminous skin, lightning calling to him through her green eyes—is forever vibrant in his memory. 2042 was the year they met, when he was twenty. She was more beautiful and real than he'd dreamed. He did not at first expect to have her heart.

Orion, as a young man, did not foresee what would come.

Even the Attractors could not find his sister, as if she no longer existed. If she was alive she must have changed her identity, completely. If she had died there was no body, no burial, no record. There was no trace.

Without remorse he is still pushing. He is organizing a book of personal philosophy. He knows the apathy of sanctuary. Yet as one who has survived he is growing wise.

He walks to the bathroom, where he pulls off his button-down pajama shirt, in front of her mirror. Almost thirty, he looks like he did just past twenty—virile, unbroken—though with less body hair. The genex are rare, but most people have been stabilized, freed from fear of diseases, from the chains of erosion, cured of ugliness through a simple procedure, a needle penetrating. It is the ultimate personal vaccine, a fundamental genetic adaptation.

SSP is a broad-scope life enhancer, perfecting the body's natural immunity with dynamic genetic code manipulation.

I always was me, no doubt, but I'm polished now. No scars. Is this face even mine? Does it speak of my memories? he wonders. Does it tell my age? Am I getting older? In the mirror is the shameless, shapeless face of modern humanity, looking back at his eyes. Something in those eyes is endless. Something in its eyes is still getting older. Something in his eyes is waiting, yet unsung.

He thinks, After all of this, in the age of immortality, at less than thirty I am somehow obsolete. Though I am the dream of millennia. Just wait.

Something new is rising—that may not much longer be known as man. We evolve a desire to evolve, and we find an incomparable method in gene extension.

If the potter is made of clay, anything is possible.

There stands a powerful man, this civilized warrior, hypnotized. Orion steps into the shower. Warm water rushes over him, over the big tiles, and he thinks for a second he should not have let Harmony go.

She will be waiting for me, in front of the TV. She'll be with me. I won't stray. Not too far.

Youth and Immortality

Harmony has gone to the kitchen, where Day is seated at the table. Her eggs are unfinished on the plate. The screen has her attention. "Good morning," Harmony says.

"Mornin'," says Day.

"You found something to eat?"

"Mmhm."

Harmony is not hungry, pouring herself some juice. Sitting, she asks, "What're you watching?"

Day answers, "It's called 'Systems Integration.'"

She follows up, "What's it about?"

Day says, as if it were a common thread, "She's half-ghost." She points. "That girl."

Harmony pauses. "Strange."

Not listening she says, "Mmhm."

Drinking her juice, Harmony asks, "Who's the actress?"

"Don't you know Sophie G? She's world famous."

"She looks familiar. So, what's the context?"

"Well she's an anarchist. Um, they thought she was in the stable, but she wasn't there anymore. Can't kill her anyway, half ghost see. She's in hangar 213." Gunshots from the TV interrupt her. "The girl makes it rain."

This gets Harmony interested, waiting.

"It's not real complicated," Day says impatiently. "She's the only one that can disarm this big time-bomb. The big guy, right there, gets her to do it, after they do it. Sorry, yeah I've seen it before but it's total obs. She doesn't die when they expect her to." She smiles, looking at Harmony for the first time in the morning. Taking a big, frustrated breath she goes on, "Spoilers! Ha. Yeah I dig it, did the first time too. Awesome photography and music, for one. They don't pull their punches. It gets pretty hard toward the end though, yeah." She looks back to the screen, saying, gesturing to emphasize, "The two of them set the world free."

"I wish I could make it rain."

Day laughs. "Yeah, us normals wouldn't have a chance in their world."

The girl has a good laugh, Harmony thinks, like a soft light. It's open like her voice—she sounds a little like dry feathers. Beneath them is a flesh-pink, and this amazes Harmony even more, realizing how they truly are a part of her, physical extensions of her body, almost like a second set of arms.

"Ummm . . ." Day shifts her focus from the movie, her feathers sliding, shifting over each other. Following Harmony's eyes she answers, "I was born genex. But they didn't come full till, maybe two years ago. Won't be full grown for two more."

"You can't even fly still, though," she says rudely, surprised by her own hostility.

Day returns with, "Can you?"

Harmony is slow to reply, "I don't care for it."

"Don't let fear stop you."

Harmony is quiet, finding no answer. When intermission comes she restarts with, "Where were you going yesterday?"

Day pauses before saying, "Here."

"Where from?"

She smiles. "Vegas." Sipping on her orange juice, she says, "I'm originally from Boulder, Colorado though. I . . . ran away years back."

Harmony listens, then, "To live with your grandpa?"

"Nah." Her smile fades. "My Graddy's a dick."

For some reason this makes Harmony laugh. Gathering her wits, she offers, "At least you have one."

"No, well that's what I call him." Explaining only a little further she says, "Foster care sucked. I ran away more than once, on my own ambition. I don't need anyone taking care of me."

After a minute Harmony notes, "You're a long way from Colorado."

Day says, "Nevada is where I was raised." Then, "I'm not the only one far from home."

Past the applestalk, out the window, hazy through a spritz of fresh water on the sill, the city is touching the sky. Harmony's valley is nowhere to be seen, though Spain is all around them. "I guess you've got a point there."

"All the same. Asturias is killer." They are silent again for a while, and Day laughs at the movie. "Your brother is weird," she says eventually.

Harmony jokes, "You're one to talk?"

Paying more attention to the screen than to Harmony, she adds, "He hardly said a word."

Harmony deadpans, "Is that hard for you?"

Day is unfazed. "He left."

"Did he say where he was going?"

"All he said is I should wait."

"Bless it," Harmony swears. She stands, combing her fingers through the front of her hair.

"What's the matter?" asks Day.

She yawns. "I don't want to lose my brother." She pauses, then, "He has chaotic fits. Clinical. You can stay here, for now. I'll come back."

"Right on," Day says flatly, sitting still. Harmony closes the outer door.

Then Day turns off the TV. Wandering into the living room, she admires the spartan décor. Day moves slowly, curious and casual. The walls are bare, save a series of animated digital landscapes on the TV. After another moment though, they bore her.

Walking down the narrow hall, she glances into Azad's messy room, smiling at his lack of civility, and looks in the closet, where the autoduster sleeps next to a stack of board games. She stops at Harmony's door. A shower runs beyond the wall, whispering. Suddenly she is hungry for an orgasm.

Fate, don't make me wait.

She enters the room with a lift of adrenaline. After taking in the bed, unmade, she peaks into the closet—very boyish—then she turns to the screen in the wall. The remote is right there. Rolling through screens quickly, from her online reblog she finds a favorite piece of Japanese erotica. She sets the scene to repeat, then turns away. Near the large bright window, atop a set of drawers, there is a group of photos in black, marbled frames. One is of Orion, near some Italian-looking buildings, smiling in a late day sun. She picks it up, looks it over, pulls the print out of the frame and hurries to put it in the pocket of her raincoat, hanging in the entry by the living room. She returns after just a few seconds, resetting the empty frame standing where it was.

The white bed is huge and so soft looking, and she does not resist it any longer. The comforter touches her skin and she shivers. She rolls across to the other side, looking at jewelry on the nightstand by the window.

Day hears when the water stops running. A minute of heartbeats later, Orion opens the door. Steam rushes around him. Water shines in the curves of his skin. A deep blue towel wraps his waist, reflecting his dark ocean-blue eyes. He sees her there, stretched out comfortably on Harmony's bed. Immediately he says nothing. A girl moans.

"I hope you don't mind me here." Silence settles as her eyes cannot help but flirt, meeting him shyly. A glow rises in her body, anticipating him. She diverts her eyes. On the television a skinny Asian girl is nude, her head shaved, bound in black tape on a couch, in a garden, while a woman with short hair runs her hand over her scalp, talking too low.

"I hope you don't mind me here," Day says again.

"No," he replies. Her silk-feathered wings spread out around her from behind, larger than he had thought, yet subtle in the grace of his vision. Her legs are slender, knees bared by olive shorts—loose at her pale waist. The smallish shape of her nipples pushes hard on the white fibers of her shirt. Her body moves with her breath. Pale hair hangs in uncombed tangles around her delicate face, and her large blue eyes reflect his. He says, "I don't mind."

This renews her confidence. Motioning casually at the screen, looking at him, she defends, "He loves her. You just don't know the story, Orion. They're a little fucked up, sure." She laughs. "But love always fucks people up. Don't you know anything about old hollywood?"

He says, "You pour water into a cracked glass. Does it leak?" She raises her eyebrows. He says, "They should untie her. Just saying. This isn't Hollywood, anyway."

"Oh. Mmmm. I think a little pain can be sexy. Sharing it. You can't be afraid to feel life. I think, well, I think anything at all is ok if they're both into it. She's totally fucking into it. I've seen this a dozen times already. Sorry."

"Maybe," he says and almost laughs. "But I'm just saying that if he loves her, he should set her free."

"How do you know that's not what he's doing?" Seeing that he is still motionless, eyeing the soft bulge of his towel, she gets up and goes casually toward him. "There are many kinds of prisons in the world."

"Yes . . ."

"Like these shorts," she interrupts, "for example." She touches his chest, sliding her fingers toward his hairless, strong navel. The girl onscreen begins to orgasm, getting louder. About Day there is a sweet aroma. Her lips smell like a painted raspberry. Orion holds her back, his hand on her collar, gently.

She coos, "I know you're not a monogamist. I looked it up." She pauses. "I can quote, 'pleasure has no consequence,'" she says and coyly smiles.

"Choices. Choices however do have consequences."

"Why?" she asks.

He walks past her, but she follows. At the closet he turns back and says, more gently, "Harmony is my lady."

"Ok." She retreats a step. Day says, hurt, "You want me to go?"

Close to Distance

Harmony knows that her raincoat is irrational, the black plastic sticking to her skin in the humid glare of winter's sun. Like her worry it is out of place. Both are habitual, shelter from the torrent—serving to lock her in.

Where is Azad?

But she knows before she sees him. He is often there, perched on the edge of life—literally straight ahead of her, on the roof of their apartment building, dangling his feet from the lip of the Earth—or so it appears to her distracted mind—watching their utopia.

The sun arcs slowly through the sky above them, casting his form as a steely silhouette to her vision, lacking any motion save the slow dance of his hair in the wind. She raises a hand to shield her eyes from the glaring lights of the glass curves in the city skyline.

The roof is empty, save two rows of raised solar panels and these siblings now between them. It is a sanctuary for Azad, looking on a tranquil sea of circles amid spires, reflecting images of the clouds and sun, of a few winged men and groups of birds.

"Azad . . ." she mutters loudly, eventually, coming up behind. "I've been looking for you, you son of a bitch."

He does not answer, and she does not expect him to, so she goes to sit beside him, just back farther from the edge.

"No need to bring mom into this," she says. He smiles, so that she knows he has heard, but does not turn his head, entranced by the city. Halcyon is of a new breed—less than ten years old. It is the golden fruit, come of the New Renaissance. The towers in the residential blocks are all the same height—grecian pillars of habitation—allowing them to see far into the distance from this perch. Now she thinks it is, in truth, the center of the world. In all directions, to the mountainous horizons, is a honeycomb of metalwork and glass, laid out in huge blocks. Atmospheric Generators tower as thin spears at intersections, piercing heaven, drawing out its energy. They grab electricity right out of the clouds, oscillator discs glinting in the light behind their sheer, sapphire-screen spear tips.

Rails curve and slowly sway, between the buildings. Catching the light, speeding past the towers, the railcars themselves are like evanescent dew on blades of grass. These rails switch and turn, moving deftly over the city heights as if alive.

The spires of the Theater sparkle in daylight, spreading out skyward an arc of epic thorns. This pierced crown adorns the day. Its brazen light reflects in the domed Coliseum and both are visible from her perch—like a sapphire-crusted tortoise-shell in the garden.

Far off in the curve of distance, nearer the center of the larger part of the system of valleys, distorted by haze and humidity, the buildings are jagged and rise toward the sun. The architecture there is more varied than in the blocks, rising to heights that humble the fifty stories upon which Harmony sits. A gyrosphere atop a thin, monolithic shaft, rotates almost imperceptibly with the moving sun, small amid the mass of buildings. The skyline of downtown Halcyon is anything but humble, curved, clean and organic, striking in glass. Amber-toned steps, small, lined with studio windows and lush with gardens, are like iron petals.

The glitter of the city in the sun is untouchable and seemingly unreal. Harmony takes in the mountains, huge in the distances, in two major rows, for the first time really in months. They are tinted gray, snow-lined beneath a fragile cobalt sky. “Beautiful day,” she comments.

A pair of jet planes is carving pale lines through the blue. She watches as they cross paths, near the spectral moon, then disappear behind a cradle of frayed gray clouds.

“Remember when we first came up here, Azad? You said you would touch the moon. I got vertigo. We should get dad out here some night. Bring Orion’s telescope. He’d love it. You would too . . . I mean I’d love it.”

There are not guardrails, but there is no danger. There is no lock on the door at the top of the stairs. There are no locks in this city. People are free here. The Strange Attractors know when they will come and what they will want. They grant every wish. The Strange Attractor satisfies every time, every single one—with a network extended through cities governing nearly nine billion worldwide.

She barely whispers, “I’m not happy, Azad.”

He turns toward her, pulling aside the hair from his face, and looks to her eyes, waiting for a reason why. It does not come. They sit for a long while in silence. The light wind, clear sun and the city surround them. Eventually she stands, turns and leaves him.

He remains there alone for most of the day, in meditation, helpless before his sight.

Pendulum Heart

It is easy to get around on the long-distance rails, and they span the continents. Two hours is an average trip across the Atlantic, undersea in the maglev tunnels, maxing at over twice the speed of sound. Harmony preferred the ride on a hover-boat ferry—for the dolphins of the Azores—but that time was years ago. Now she has not left Halcyon in many months. She will not today. The Pyramids stand, still.

Between the Holiday Malls and the silver dome of the rail station, her grocer is a large gray flat. Yet it is a center of activity. People swarm the parks nearby. They play games with checkered balls, or loiter at dark opal fountains, eating, smoking, drinking and a couple are fucking, pale in the sun.

Harmony moves among them, not the only one wearing a coat. She is in no hurry to get home. Stopping in the park she watches a soccer game for children. Their intrinsic vitality, coupled with poor strategy, forces her smile. What's in that ball? she wonders. Grass stains and giggles notwithstanding, these are the born genex and their power is odd. Like a wild thing a little boy runs barefoot, gaunt, faster than would seem natural. Another kid exudes remarkable strength. One small girl moves with the instincts of a savannah cat, her wild black mane reinforcing the image. It is a layman's shorthand, referring to them as hybrids, derogatory to science that has moved far past animal models—and these look like normal children, essentially, unlike the earlier extended ones, or the gothic freak gangs of the thirties. Now one stumbles. Getting to his feet, he is laughing and a notion strikes her as unsettling . . . they are children. Small flying cameras watch the field.

In '29 she was seven. Harmony had a very different life, though the mountains have not moved. There was no city here in Asturias, no Halcyon. Azad was her only friend, save the elderly neighbors. She ran the endless hills, owned the woods with him, exploring their father's land. Playing games of hide and seek, or chasing birds, pretending to be soldiers—their pastime was discovery. Their sitter, when Mrs. King was out, was the sun, with a warm kiss for dirty elbows, bright laughter and frayed jeans.

She remembers that sun was high and the grass was tall. It must have been spring; the colors across her memory were lush. Puddles shone in the uneven earth, and the air smelled of morning rain.

Humming In-A-Gadda-Da-Vida she wandered over the hills. She remembers a purple butterfly crossing her path. She made a game of being lost, then found by a rich alien who gave her super powers. Cresting a long climb, her hardy calves aching, she came to an unknown territory. A small clearing opened in front, beneath a rocky hill. Yellow light shone through the stands of trees, marking a road. She realized, tired, that she was far from home. With hunger in her belly she sat, her back against a great, winding old tree—her eyes watering as the sun went down.

Returning to humming, calming herself, she was in the middle of the song when something in the shadows moved. Sitting up straight now she held her breath. It emerged—not more than a pup but nearly as large as she. Its black eyes were glowing, lit by fear, and she held perfectly still as it crept cautiously forward. Muscles tensed beneath gray fur as it stepped, looking at her. Harmony closed her eyes. There was a noise of leaves.

When she opened them, the wolf was gone. In front of her now was a skinny boy. His long hair was blond. In dirty torn jeans and no shirt, his tan chest was scratched red, as if by branches. Harmony watched him in awe. She knew him before he ever said his name. With a shy hand he helped her from the ground, giving a strange sort of grin. She kissed him once on the cheek, feeling thankful. He did not kiss her back, but his smile bloomed in a blush as he wordlessly turned away.

With him, Harmony shared her aching heart, years passing like a wind full of imagination, into adolescent rebellion. They grew, loving experimentalists, misfits with untamed spirits—immature, they were dramatists. As similar waves they amplified.

That first day they teased.

By the time they were sixteen, they went often into the luminous dark, the night life, but even when she was passing twenty, her view of the outside world was shaped much like her father's widescreen TV. She was isolated from war, safer on high ground when the ocean began to rise. She was apart from the hungry, partitioned by the grace of god and television. Asturias was peaceful and free. The refugees, the dying must be part of a plan she could not comprehend—the casualties, as the wars, were not her own. Behind this veil she felt helpless, more so as she grew up.

Yet the snows of Asturias were beautiful.

In '42, Harmony was twenty. The Attractors rose with a new sun, uniting nations in a Unified Earth. The science was not in her language, but her Spain like a flower bloomed when the transition came.

Harmony signed petitions against Halcyon, but it was larger. Her dad sold his land, and there was nothing she could do but watch, and hate him for it. She went barefoot through the woods like a witch, talking to the trees and to god.

In only months the valley was totally, irreversibly transformed. Some days she watched the construction with Sayd, standing on a sheer cliff, looking over the expanse. The scrapes on his chest had turned black, to tribal tattoos, branching in thorns on his arms. His spiked hair was dyed blue that summer. They smoked opium and dreamed out loud. They made love in the sunlight. Even she could not deny that the construction was a miracle, a crystal in metamorphosis—organic and robotic, hardly a worker seen.

The city blocks rose.

A massive ellipse of tents and RVs spiderwebbed away from the domes. Five hundred thousand bonfires dotted the valley floors at night. Refugees of wars and disasters were gathering. Ragged migrants looked on with hungry eyes and began to pray, in large groups, under the stars. As the skeletons of Halcyon's buildings grew endless, automated from the dirt, the migrants said with hope to each other, Finally we're coming home.

Like a phase transition, water suddenly turning to ice, soon they were in apartments, eating well, with 3D televisions and surround-sound speakers in their walls, games and communications connected to global networks, automatic dishwashers, refrigerators and perfect, clean water. It was—they were—suddenly free. Paradise thrust upward, now upon them, a fountain.

When Sayd's half-brother first came to town, in these same cyclone years, he seemed to her the avatar of a new era. Renaissance shone like revolution, fresh as the stars in his blue eyes. Through his telescope she touched imagination—Saturn's crown, Olympus Mons and endless, emotionless void. He told her how he wanted to see other stars.

He pointed at the cold sky and said, See those seven stars there? Tracing with his finger he said, My sword.

She laughed, Are you drunk? That's clearly a butterfly.

But every time she saw the night sky Orion was there.

Sayd was desperate for her love. He was in the very first group of genex jaggers in Halcyon, at the top of his class. His noble heart wore a badge as if it were a birthmark. His bravery, selflessness and strength were unbound, everything police should have been, if they rarely were. His play, to show his worth to her, was adolescent but true to the core.

Still a rookie, months in, he came home with somebody else's blood dry on his hands. It was a girl he could not save. Exactly what happened she never knew, even today. She yelled at him but he was unmoved. Depression took him.

Yet she was saved from his ruin.

As he fell away from her, she held on to Orion.

She was there when Sayd almost killed him.

Now she thinks of him, often, despite the pass of years. Her distance from her memory smooths its flaws. He was a freak long before those changes, even as a child masochistic, hypersexual. They had a lot in common.

She was not without her own mistakes, as it was.

Orion, my cup of sky, what have we become?

Does my past matter as this new day carries on?

Children run on genex manicured grass—dark green and damp. They chase their checkered ball with the force of a millennium. When they catch it they kick it away too quickly, or someone else takes it. They keep moving, oxygen pumping to their brains and making them whole. The boy's face is set, Harmony is thinking. He really wants the fucking ball. The power of science, glory of art, the endurance of muscle—for balls. The epic, unique tragedy of history was a preamble to this kids' soccer game. What is in that sphere?

Sunlight?

Harmony turns away.

As she passes some colorful punks, playing cards, the wide gray block before her is not marvelous, though soothing, surrounded by park where once there would have been parking lots. As she crosses into the grocery, through its big open doors, music hums. She tries to hum with it, but does not feel it. Beethoven I think, whatever not his best but timeless. Like cucumbers, eggs. She takes stick butter and bread, cranberry juice in a glass jar and an issue of Popocu. Bubble Resort on the Moon, says the cover. She smiles big for the first time today, taken by a graphic of low-g waterslides, flipping pages, imagining lunar volley ball.

She leaves, after stacking her things into bags marked with a chaos butterfly and walks through the large open door under an imposingly bright sun.

There are no cashiers; there is no cash. There are no service-people, though a bot is anchored near the door, polite. Everything in the market is free, openly. Products come from automatic lines. Atoms rearrange in highly ordered chains, molecules bend to the nanoassembly protocol, and gold comes of straw. Nothing is wasted. The autodusters, streetsweepers and the Attractors' unfailing heart recycle all. It is perpetual living. Costs have been reduced to nearly nothing, and the machines continue to pay this price, with the regenerative powers of Earth and sun, nearly limitless.

The technology was built on thousands of years of history, but what came of the womb of the industrial revolution was an anti-economy, the dissolution of demand by the maturity of production. Quality and innovation became the largest market forces in the cities of the New Renaissance.

Harmony walks toward home, bags weighing down her hands, raincoat keeping her from getting dry, and part of her continues to dream. The fire in Sayd's eyes looked right into her when she was seven—he gave her his hand in exchange for her heart. She still cannot let go. Orion's starlit gaze held her last night. For a moment now I am alone. The ocean of my soul is quiet. Oh loves. Give me a wish, give me a reason, she begs, almost vocal. Let me breathe! I must exhale.

Hush darling, redoubts her iron mother.

Relax, child, play.

Nothing is required of you.

Glacier and Diamond

Firelit, pale gold surrounds his large black pupils, brightening his narrowed eyes. His lashes are flecked with orange. His nose is thick, the taut skin of his cheeks olive-toned but marked with a few freckles. Biting down on the filter of a cigarette, the curve of his mouth bears just a hint of the years he has seen.

Her voice comes, soft. "Sayd," says the girl with subtle rose cheeks and lavender hair, setting her drink on the coffee table, kneeling next to him in the dark. "What is it? You've been out here all morning."

"Violet," he replies, not looking at her, "leave me be." She stays, though she quiets. Sayd is overcome by the history, coming like a river over its banks. He closes his eyes, only to see his seven-year-old Harmony, her back against that winding tree on the rocky hillside, under blooming stars, big clouds.

Sayd asks, whispering, "Can we protect them?"

Violet answers with, "Who?"

He swallows. "My brother."

After a moment she asks, "From?"

"Last night Faith came by. Warned me."

Quietly she says, "Is it fucked up?"

"Yes. We need to change it."

Violet asks, hesitant, "Can we?"

Sayd does not respond.

Then enters a girl with shiny red hair, turning on the light, holding a breakfast sandwich. She says, making a vertical mark in the air with two fingers, "Birth is the last tragedy."

Violet says, "You don't know, Scarla."

"Oh?" she answers, not looking. Sayd does not answer them, putting out his cigarette halfway through and looking to the door. Immediately Scarla says, "He lives." Her sarcasm is not apparent, so she adds, ironic, cheering up, "Death would be a garnish. Cry goodbye, Satan." After another pause she laughs a little and says, "I can see through you, Sayd. Are you seriously still going to the TLA today?"

He stands. As he hastily pulls on his black raincoat Violet opens her mouth but is silent. Sayd exits.

At the street he stops, unsure. A cloud obscures the sun. Cold wind comes past. A black car draws smoothly to a stop in front of him. A small family emerges laden with baggage. Two adults and a toddler, they have black hair, white skin, gills in their necks. The little one bobbles, forward, balancing against the weight of her luggage. Her hair drips over a gray raincoat. The taxi's door remains open after they are past, and Sayd slides into the empty seat. With no driver the car rolls out, quickly joining in the flow of traffic.

Eyes closed he moderates his breathing. Memories are following him, so he allows another one now.

They hiked in wooded hills, through the calm of recent snow shadowed by the city's evening glow, gray with clouds and stars. They were looking for a tree, and the young pine they came before was reaching, full, frosted. Harmony spoke, and her voice came through his shell like nothing else could, It's just rebellion. We're born innocent. These inane traditions. She smiled, mumbling the next bit, "Well, Dad wants it. Poor thing has roots." Her green eyes in the shadow of her hood looked at him. The snow was lessening. Night was creeping under the bark of the trees. She declared, softly, "Our crime is only proof of our innocence." Now she giggled audibly. With a glance to the pale, cotton sky she finished, "Celebrate life, decorate the dead."

Azad smiled and said, "You're insane."

"Am I?" She looked at him. "Dad used to say that."

"Yeah I know."

Orion offered, "It's not a mana tradition."

"You don't get it. He was raised with Christmas trees. Anyway, so he likes to study world religions? Would you just let me do this for him?"

An animal nearby made itself known then with a whimper, startling them all. In the quiet and cold somehow it had approached without a sound, though it was not a wild thing but a house dog, at a glance. Wet fur clung to its hungry ribs. Sayd knelt, to whistle, but their mere attention seemed to frighten it and it took off, fast and light into the woods.

None of them spoke. Stepping back, Sayd pulled a fireman's axe from the inside of his raincoat. With a resonant, sharp and wet noise, he cleaved into the tree. The blade stuck. He wrenched it out with a movement of his shoulder. Harmony stood near, watching the penetrating night. Each of the many swings that followed brought a thundercrack. In the mountain stillness the thick wood splintered with a sudden, powerful rattle, breaking under its own weight.

The snowfall was dissolving to rain.

Hours later, water was silently tapping against the shaded window in her father's large apartment. In the upper pines of the tree a circle of fake doves was perched, below the high ceiling. Young and full, shining lights from deep shades of green, its smell mingled with a jasmine incense. The streaming music was a slow jazz, rolling with timbales. A poet read beside a saxophone, somber, "Given need, my will divides. In time. I will form feathers of the ashes, ashes of my wings."

Her dad was out, at a show she sent him to, while they stood and decorated the tree. Then they reclined for a while, everyone but Sayd sharing a vapor pipe. The air was thick with it when Sayd's phone buzzed, in his pocket. He cracked a smile as he pulled it out, buzzing again.

His memory fragments at the sound, like a storm, thrusting him forward, inevitably.

Harmony's shirt was lifted, up from her hip as she lay back on the couch, with Sayd coming into the apartment. Orion's belt was loose. They moved too quickly as he stood in the doorway.

It was not shock that twisted then, a fire ignited in his chest, or simple anger. It was like molten steel in his lungs, betrayal.

Yet it was not in that moment that he lost her but weeks before, and he knew it even then.

He unfastened his coat, shrugging it off. It thudded with the weight of his axe. He walked to Orion. Their eyes did not break contact.

As he reached in, grabbing his shirt, Orion pushed his hands aside, trying to get off the couch. Sayd lunged at him, bracing his forearm under Orion's chin and pinning him to the cushions. Shrugging off Harmony's hands he pulled him up by the neck, lifting him clear of the sofa. Awkwardly Orion's jeans fell from his waist, but he had only a second to struggle against the grip as in one motion Sayd threw him into the wall. Spider-webbing cracks spread through it. Sayd turned to Harmony, who was screaming at him, and Orion got up on his knee, trying to pull up his pants. Then he came back at him, opening Orion's cheek and his knuckles. The rumbling saxophone swelled.

The call on his phone could have been innocent, but it was not. He often blamed it for the whole day.

It was a page from the precinct, calling him in. No choice but to answer, taking him to the hall. He heard Harmony giggling as he shut the apartment door behind, and his grin expanded. Walking toward the elevator, he was cursing under his breath, to shake off the smile. The elevator was late, coming from the lobby floor. Oh, he thought, I left my wallet on the table. It'll be right on time. He jogged back.

Blood spat, out the left side of Orion's mouth. The jags burst through the front door, left ajar. Without pause they tazed Sayd in the back, grabbing him with gloved hands and pulling him away from his brother. Colorless fire surged through his body. Energy, sharp like knives, pulsed in from his spine. For only a second it silenced even his mind.

Harmony was quiet—her eyes were wet—as they hauled him out into the black night. The last he remembers, until he awoke in restraints in his gray-stone cell, is the blood on his hands, streaked up his tattooed arm, fast to get cold in the thin orange hairs on his knuckles.

Time did not forgive him.

He returned from prison a shadow.

The needles came back, genex injections and the ink, to finish what they had started. The laws allowed for felons to be chipped, like jags, with circuits as a safety measure. When did the torture and the metamorphosis begin, exactly? Did it end? These are things the butterfly never knows. These scars, he would come to say, my lacerations, they've turned into my wings.

They never made me strong enough to change the past. Put an animal in my DNA. Sometimes, I think, that griffon's in my mind. I want to let it out. I can't get it out.

They released him from prison but couldn't set him free.

Orion will not be ok.

But Harmony . . .

Breathes.

In fact.

She's going to need me.

Are we helpless? he wonders.

He opens his eyes as the taxi stops. The door opens, and stepping out onto the walk he looks up at Orion's apartment building. Flicking a light for his cigarette he pauses then for the tattooed Eye of Ra on the back of his hand. Raising his palm to the higher windows, as if blocking out his brother, he exhales smoke that swirls past his fingers.

They have not trusted each other since that day.

Sayd's memories run still when his eyes are open, and as he thinks back on that time, even it is just one night in a river of nights. Death and love come and pass, but his is an epic longing, underscoring the entire fall of time.

I would never have hurt him if I hadn't failed her already. They had to reconstruct his jaw. For the coldness of reality, I punished Orion.

It was only days before when I saw that young girl. What befell her. The blindness of the earth.

The moon rose too fast, damp and lonely at her back. The dark old man grabbed her. Was he using her as a shield? Before I was ready, out of nowhere came the judgment, that old scientist, and he gave no apologies for his timing. Between cold sniffles he didn't have much to say. That old angel brought me to my knees with four words, slithered out of his throat like a ghost.

There is no justice.

Repeat this until you understand.

That wasn't Harmony, Sayd is thinking.

It is a fit of imagination. As the taxi departs behind him Sayd realizes why he must have come.

Bent Wings

The apartment is softly lit. As she sips at a glass of water, her even voice contrasts the tension in her words. Faith says, "We're in a feedback loop."

He wants to speak but struggles in silence.

She says quickly, "It's ok though because I was insane."

"No," he says, rising to his feet. "I just need more details." At her silence he turns on her, angry, "Or why the hell did you tell me?"

Faith looks past him. Her voice is quiet. "I didn't sleep. Going over these conversations. Hoping to find something." She stops, tasting the idea, "There is just one path. You know things only happen once right? Leaves turn to the sun. Everything is what it is." She puts her hand up. "Sayd, I've mined your thoughts. I've told you that our brother is dying. And your thought is still about me, sexually, right now while we're speaking." She grins unhappily. "We're machines. I mean not your coherent thoughts, but yes, you can't keep a straight line if his life depended on it. There's hardly an impulse in you beyond an animal."

Sayd is looking at the window, through which the sun is raining, intensely in white. He slowly says, "It's a mistake."

"No," she corrects. "It's not."

"I'll stop the whole damn game."

She goes on, "You won't. There's nothing to save him from. The rule is CE. His choices are legal." Her lips stay parted.

He mutters, "We're missing something."

Her voice steadies. "Are we?" Rising, she refills her glass with water from the tap. Then, "Actually I have too much." She smiles unhappily, pouring it back, "We probe galaxies, Sayd. How come we can't find what's right behind our eyes? Will," she says the word with sadness. "That's the grail." Lifting the pint glass to her lips she takes a long swallow of water.

Sayd has calmed. "Parliament can change the future. That's the whole basis of their control."

Frustration fills her voice, "Jags don't change a thing. How can you not know this. Being as you were one. Listen to me. The Attractor is a part of the world. So, it effects its own predictions. But a causal loop doesn't actually loop, not really. It just goes. And at this hour the chain is thoroughly adjusted. Our choices have been calculated. It well knows what I am saying now and has since the attosecond I turned away. Occam's paradox prevents me from watching my own future, but it does nothing to stop the Attractor." Her anger breaks free for a few sentences, "Do you fucking get it? The choice is Orion's. Though I try. Oh I plant your god damn roses!" Then she looks away, saying dryly, "I will tell him." The next words seem to bite, into her, "I have no choice. This isn't about me," she says, tearing. "Of course I will tell him." Sayd stands, without another word. Then he is gone.

Faith stares at the kitchen walls, holding the thin hem of her knee-length skirt.

Her thoughts caught up in the web of chance and choice, circling out into incoherence, she tries simply to quiet her shouting mind.

Soon though Orion comes through the door with a young girl. Faith flinches back a slow step, into the counter, from their cloud colors, watching from the kitchen while they stand in the living room unaware of her. "Don't laugh at me." Day smiles, pouting.

Orion laughs, "Sounds pretty gross though, in fairness."

"You don't eat with your ears, kid," she says, tugging once at her own lobe. Then, "But maybe I do mean raspberry. I'd eat almost anything. At least with peanut butter I would. I'm hungry."

Faith comes to the doorway, saying nothing.

The winged one greets her quickly, palm up, "Hi."

Faith says just, "Orion," watching as he goes to his bedroom. Now she looks to Day, who stayed behind, and says, "You don't even know him."

Day wipes at her eye. Faith looks through her, and she interlaces her fingers. Her wings flutter helplessly and Day says, "Orion was actually just telling me he wants you to come with us." A big Labrador precedes him from the bedrooms—a black silk beast, muscled under thick fur. It continues past them into the kitchen. Now the whirling clicks of its feeder are heard.

"Come watch the tournament?" Orion asks.

Faith answers immediately, as if sick, "No. Come with me to the Iris?"

His smile fades at her sarcasm. "Ok then, but really it should be a good match. Biggest one this month."

"Every time." Her eyes are moist, reflecting yellow sunlight from the window. Her words come uncertainly, stumbling a little, as if fighting themselves. For a few seconds she selfishly clings to his innocence. "Stay home. Don't play."

He says, "I'll be home tonight."

She hesitates, as if words would make it real. "Don't do the TLA today. You're better than that stupid game."

"I'm too modest for that," he jokes. She does not laugh. "I'm already way late. People are waiting for me. You should come."

Desperation creeps in as she finds herself struggling against an invisible wall. "You think you're a star but you're not. We're nobody." His smile falls. She thinks, the scene is already done. "You could do something real, Orion."

His patience slips. "Exactly what?"

Without knowing why, she says, overflowing with pain, "Bring our sister home."

He pauses to look in her eyes. Plainly he says, "I don't know any better than you where she is." He emphasizes, letting out, "The hard truth is she doesn't want to be found." He looks away. "Anyway the TLA is just one of the things I'm doing. Sis you know already. I'll have that manuscript for you soon."

She looks at the floor, breathing it out, "You will die."

His voice rises, "I won't bring back the dead!"

"No really you won't." Almost silently she breathes, stubbornly, "You're going to." Then she looks up, the words of her message like venom. "Today. An accident in the TLA."

The silence that follows stretches out for an unmeasured time. He does not answer or question, but stands open before her, waiting. Then Faith wetly blinks, and when she opens her eyes he has turned away. Words catch in her throat.

Day hesitates, looking from her to him. Then she also is leaving. Through her tears, by the feathers of wings Faith is struck with an uncontrollable, inappropriate awe. On her back this girl bears flight, but it is as if stolen, on a beggar, belonging truly to time, to scientists and minds she could never imagine. She has no clue about their desperate crawl, this pale dream, evolution's epic goal, she. Faith wonders how well an apple may ever understand a tree. We are so small.

The door Orion closes is quiet, just normal in her ears.

"Don't go." Did I say it? Did he hear me? Is it too late? She sits on the cyan couch, struggling for an instinct that will not come. It is her belief—it is scientific fact—that she is helpless. Yet something in this pain is like a crack in her walls, a wind breathing on her will. When he goes all is lost. Some part of her believes he might return—some deaf, crying axiom—because the world itself must go with Orion. He is the part of it that breathes. This causes her to rise, pulling on her raincoat, a reflection of blue sky. Yet she does not follow him. Faith moves toward the rail, the halls of the Iris.

Reflections

The UFT was uncovered in 2017, five years before Harmony's birth. Her father was in isolation, studying eastern thought, spending much of his time in meditation. Sitting on a wooden block, in an open field of tall yellow grass, palms turned to a cresting sunrise over the treeline, as if in photosynthesis, he watched the shadows play behind closed eyes. When his cellphone rang it was with a birdsong, and it took him some time to answer. The news was deceptively small, much like a viral seed: a paper was published, an experimental series verified, proving a theorem about gravity and its translation on subatomic scales. He would not remember hanging up the phone. Instead he remembers only a sensation of that bright day, of the warmth of dawn and a vague sense of awesome foreknowing that he would later compare to a ray, red on closed eyes.

Many scientific groups claimed to have created the Unified Field Theory, simultaneously. Hackers and nationalized cells all raced to put it to use. Born of the realization that the disparity in their two theories was the key to their unification, it is beautiful to the trained mathematician, divine to a man like her father, gracefully simple yet infinite in consequence. To most it is a mystery, useless as an atom. The Strange Attractor is the application of this theory.

Its core is one atom of hydrogen in a two-story metal sphere, at the center of their city. It is the oracle, a pearl heart to the modern world. It is the chaos butterfly, as it hovers, unraveling destiny's web.

That hydrogen appears motionless at the center of the SA Complex, in a gyrospheric vacuum of light, but it is not. In constant flux, it cannot be still.

Light pulses from the sensors of the Attractor, rotating in four dimensions at intervals of attoseconds, and the atom is like a prism, casting a many-colored shadow. The mainframes model it and slow it, tracing its fields, and by tracking only measured positions, are able to solve for the unknown velocities, creating a perfect, evolving map of the atom as it was moments before. It is not necessary to separate it from its environment. It is not finite. Volumes of data come forth.

It bears an impression of the weight of the cosmos. It is infinite in possibility. A butterfly's breath, taken, alters the balance of the earth—like a pond rippling in rain.

Like a needle to a record the SA translates the world.

Through a network of Strange Attractors, particles and waves across the surface of the Earth are modeled and fed into the Unified Theory. A map is extrapolated to the next, from the present into the near future.

In 2051 this chaos horizon, where processing speed crosses with error-checking and raw potentiality, for most of the world, is at twenty-four hours. Aided by additional models, hypothetical maps, psychological Web Theory and external, real-world measurements, the SA Network changed everything.

With this crystal came dominion.

Supported by the scientific and military complex of the United Nations, early Strange Attractors proved more influential than atomic bombs in deciding on national histories. Their surveillance indicated exactly where insurgents were likely to attack, and hypothesis models showed how the UN might react. The effect was peaceful, devastating. In a span of years the network spread nearly everywhere, followed closely by the establishment of a representative Parliament for the Unified World.

These revolutionary impacts of the UFT were unexpected by most. Harmony's father did not see them coming.

Yet he was not blind.

Crosslegged in a sunlit field, soaking energy through his pores, echoing a cellphone message through the sacred hall of his soul, he felt for a powerful meditative second the truth behind their numbers, that unifying thing within everything that is nothing—that is not energy or matter, but method. Like amino acid to a tree, the archaic symbols in the scientists' formula bore little resemblance to their consequence. Divided only by the space of time, transformed in reflection but more than casually similar, they are made one by the thread of method—like rain and clouds, or shadows and dawn.

Opening Light

In the blue sky Orion lets go, for a moment. Different paths open before him. There are many people passing in all directions between them and the rail station, a busy day expanding, their bodies just like particles to the universe. The light is hard, casting shadows and silhouettes. Day has gone just a little ahead of him. There is a big man, with long black hair, off in the crowd, and for a second he thinks it is Azad. When he looks at Orion it is clearly not him. This guy is much older. He walks off.

Faith enters a long, curved hallway. The high, arched wood paneling is lit by crystal spheres, hanging on long, thin gold chains. It is known as the Hall of Eyes, circling the Iris. Faith goes alone now, formal, a long white coat over her clothes, down this whispering corridor. A spiral stair disappears into the polished wood wall. In one of dozens of enclaves she removes her workcoat, hanging it on the tall chair. Taking a seat at her desk, she dons a wireless headset, ocean blue, which she has customized with manga tentacle stickers.

First there is nothing as she closes her eyes. She relaxes her mind, focusing her thoughts. The AI systems sense her, analyzing the patterns of activity in her brain, locating thoughts that match personalized templates in its command database. A message writes out in electric grays, streaming text in her closed eyes. It is literal only in her mind:

SEA[D3[09:00:00 ; 50392.- ; 65087.- ; 3'5 ; Orion]]

Prophets, deeper in the compound, compiling her coded request from independent mainframes, return identical results to her, only seconds later.

1[subject: Orion, RWYLH]

2[object highlight: 99]

3[temp: -22]

Add Parameter?

She thinks: MAP[VIS[RAI 15' ; VEC: His eyes]]

Vividly, but in grayed colors a scene is crafted, projected into the theater of her mind's eye. In layers it comes into focus, inducing a touch of vertigo, as if she were no longer at the enclave. Orion lay horizontal. He wears a jumpsuit, blue, blackened, burnt. His eyes and mouth are closed. It is one still, almost monochrome frame, and so it is not surprising when he does not breathe. The room is otherwise empty. Its smooth walls fade to black fifteen feet from Faith's view. He lay on a metal cart. Medical tubes trace from his wrists to a canister and mechanical device beneath him. They run with a silver fluid.

The Prophets' request is psychic, gray:

New Parameter?

SCAN[08:00:00 – 10:00:00]]

MAP[VIS[RAI 15' ; VEC: Harmony]]

A series of images begins to appear, like a dream from an old movie projector, almost instantly.

In a scene like transparent animation cells overlaid, Harmony is rendered as a blur of motion, hooking from the corners of her trailing raincoat to her black silhouette, ending at the door. In the center of this activity she stands still for many minutes, and there the thin white oval of her face is clear, her cheekbones, as with her dark eyes. One of her hands extends, pale as a ghost, from these midnight shapes.

CLR, Faith thinks. The image scatters.

There is a question in her mind, a fleck of dust to her like a shadow on the sun. Pain comes with this, a yearning in her tired heart, bearing sharpness, weight. Guilt's a cancer, and an obsolete concept, she thinks. A relic of poor circuitry. Why can't I get rid of this pain? Time. Choices gone before I would ever see them. If I hadn't known? If I hadn't warned him at all?

When she thinks about Orion even in this moment it is with reverence. With his intuition, his drive, Orion is the lit urban day, immortal. When Amber was around he always had a book in his hand.

Last night, hours before the decision came down from the Judge, the Interpreters knew well what it would be: The laws of Competitive Exception apply. Orion is aware of his fate. As soon as the Iris highlighted the object, it was a breach of protocol for her to see it without oversight, but it was inevitable still that she would.

She thinks, RENDR ANIMATE[NOW]

Deep in the Iris is a dark, large room. Prophets wear black suits with white dress shirts and blue ties. They are plugged into their screens, with bloodless lips under headsets. Translating Attractor data into the shapes of reality, locating specific elements in that sea, and linking these together, chaining hypotheticals, is their life. This is why the first Attractors—prototyped in secret in 2019, closely following the discovery of the Unified Theory—were hardly more than novelties. Therefore crime in most of the world did not end until 2043.

Four thousand Prophets watch the Iris of Halcyon. Their minds are augmented with electronic circuits.

Thin tubes run from their pant legs into the floor. Their emotions are offline. They serve like an optic nerve, without which the Iris is but a dead receptor—the many Interpreters a deaf cortex.

The Attractors are learning at every moment, adding to the World Database, evolving. In this massively autonomic system, billions of commands are sent daily without any Judges' oversight. Human Prophets cannot maintain that pace. They need not. Society has been stabilized.

Still the Iris and its Prophets are constant in their analysis. They live in the future, experiencing so many hypothetical worlds, cyberpaths chatting through instant mail and groupspeak. Their curiosity swells as tomorrow unveils, in zeros sparking ones that move with flesh and blood.

One of them reacts out of rhythm with this room. She leans back into her form-fitted chair. Tension reveals in her shaking, bony hands, feeling for a release on the sides of the black headset.

The chair responds with a hiss of pressure released. Detaching from her wrists, tubes retract into holes. She bleeds, small trails. Finally, the headset lifts away.

She stands in the half-light, unsteadily bracing on her chair. The room is very dark, dimly lit by electronic screens. Illegible without the headgear, they give a faint yellow glow. Seventy-nine Prophets sit, half-whispering, at their stations. She takes a small pencase, or something of that shape, from her desk and puts it in her pocket. As she takes a step away from the chair her posture straightens. In the round halogen, her bony, emaciated arm scarcely casts a shadow.

A tangle of light hair runs down her back, spilling open, long to her hip.

Through an automatic doorway she passes into total darkness, continuing forward slowly as if sleepwalking, conscious for a time only of a steady descent. One by one, her steps eventually fill hours.

Brightly, a young girl lies in the grass, on a long hill under thick skies, an inch of snow gathering around her, layering on her chest. There is blood trailing from her hairline. Icy feathers protrude from inside of her loose raincoat. A man in black rises behind her.

A man with long dark hair waits at the terminal for a railcar that runs late.

The Prophet keeps going, coming into a new light. She is blinded suddenly by the expanse, but this does not stop her.

As her vision clears she finds that the apparent sun is but a steady glow, cast through ventilation shafts into a huge, dark, metal-reinforced stone cavern. Magnetic rail conveyors cross her path overhead and on both sides, in many directions, over great stone ramps. Crates hover past. A huge windowed container flies by, like a yacht off in the dark, full of spidery metal. She keeps moving forward, walking barefoot on cold stones.

Coil

The Coliseum at Halcyon is built of synthetic marble and stained glass, seating two hundred thousand patriots, give or take, in massive red bleachers, beneath a dark, huge dome. A statement, extramodernist, with big, black tribal sculptures, its pillars, polished and thick, appear both ancient and eternal. It is more than the wildest things most architects imagine. If their labor was unchained and their productive power was limitless, still their paradigm would crack with the potential of the Coliseum. It is an arena for genex competition, in new games, for the modern voyeur with the latest toys. It looms atop the hill, like a huge, crowned beast, covered entries looking down open paths.

Orion approaches. It is a short distance from the rail gate, with Day beside him. They come over marble paths toward a sea of people. Orion bears a sharp demeanor, taller than many of the spectators. A few seem to recognize him. Baseball-size drones hover and zip through the air, a couple remaining around these two, but quiet at a distance. "So I flushed all his hard drugs," Day is saying, rubbing her bare arms in the sunlight. Her feathers ruffle. "He locked me in the cellar, you know. No shit. I had to get rid of them anyway. Some things mix, some don't."

They move into a dense throng of people, massive under the arch, and Day grabs his forearm, not to be separated in the current. They find a small vacant spot by the wall, close enough together that they may keep from yelling over the crash of cheers.

He says, "Faith is wrong, this time."

Day hesitates. "But she's a Prophet, right?"

"No, Faith is an Interpreter." It comes to him easy for a second to explain something familiar. "Prophets don't choose. That's the difference. They are slaves to the truth. Faith decides what questions to ask." A proud upturn appears on his lips. "And how to make sense of it all." Surprisingly what he feels most at this moment is something deep released—a great tension unwinding, like a huge steel coil.

"It's wild," she says softly.

A face draws Orion's attention. Sayd approaches, in a black hood, deep tribal tattoos dark across his chest. Scarla and Violet are with him, both dressed in shades of red. Day is silent as she follows Orion's eyes. She sees Sayd for the first time.

"Hello, Orion." His mouth betrays a half-risen smile. "Hello, Farfall." Blond and orange hair spikes out from the edges of his hood. He is awesome in vulgarity. Day blushes at his acknowledgement of her, though she knows not what the name he called her means.

When Orion speaks he asks directly, reading his brother's eyes, "You talked to Faith?"

Scarla beside him, anxious, looking away, Sayd says, earnest, his voice calm, "I want to fix things between us." He extends an inked, sharp-nailed hand. "We might be brothers again. Let's walk away from this, man. Let's go get a juice, or something. You know?"

Scarla says, "That's not a bad plan."

"I won't forgive you." Orion's words cut through.

Sayd withdraws. "I didn't ask you to."

Orion says, straight, "But I won't play. I've already called ahead and canceled."

Violet comes behind and grabs Scarla with one hand, by the upper arm, directing her words to Orion. Her voice shakes, "You could still listen."

A group of teenagers cuts between them, impolitely brushing past, chasing each other in laughter. Orion watches them pass before saying, "People used to be mortal. Living life in fear of death." Echoing roars of the crowd fill the stadium. Orion waits, then when the noise has subsided says, "We aren't." Speaking slower, stubborn, fighting the cognitive dissonance of competing ideas, he says, "I didn't come here to play. She saved my life, I guess, right? Money doesn't carry her phone. And we meet at the elevator, every time."

Sayd's voice is calm, volcanic. "We're long past the chaos horizon." His breath grows very heavy. "You want to know what I think? I think you won't back down." For a distinct, empty moment he stands there, fighting self-control. "That's basically what Faith said. You just can't submit. Always too good to consider yourself human." He moves into the crowd.

Orion is shaking when Day looks back toward him. Her angel shape hits him like a sun, and suddenly he does not want to share this moment with her, like this. "Don't be a tourist." She winces. He reacts, offering, "The whole world is built on it. As basic, as important as what goes up must come down, we make choices." Frustrated, he reasons, "I am not a stone. The Attractor knows it." He adds, "You familiar with Occam's Paradox?" Day shakes her head. "History is always a straight line. Knowing the future changes it." She looks at him blankly. He explains, "Self-awareness makes prophecy impossible, that's really what it means, even for the SA. It changed, in that very breath when she talked to me. If anything the paradox is an argument against free will, I'll tell you. It's just that things don't happen twice. Faith warned me. The Attractor saved me. That's what it's for. Nothing here is hardly dangerous, even if I did play. I train for this four days a week." He laughs. "I mean you've seen me on TV. I live for this game."

Orion is in the locker room, surrounded by his teammates. The two closest are a pony-tailed and a butch-cut girl, strong in custom tracksuits, fitted tight. Electrodes run visibly throughout, intricate with circuit designs. His TLA suit is basic, hanging in his locker. His helmet sits above it on the shelf, on top of his four shock limiting rings and the SLR belt pack. He pulls a glove on, then takes it off.

Gradually his team files out to the elevator room.

He looks up to see Day coming from near the exit, lit from behind now, just a few feet away. She says, playful, "The fuck are you doing then?"

Dangerously, he feels the coil unwinding in his soul grow tense. A moment of natural stillness follows. "Waiting for Harmony to show." He says, "Wondering if memory is immortal."

Day shrugs lightly. "Well I came from heaven to save you from silly prophecy," she says, unfolding her wings and smiling. "Come here." He does. Orion follows her words. Even so he intends to hold her back.

Grabbing his waist with both hands she pulls herself in.

She breathes against him, her shape a counterpoint to his. Everything in existence is in that wave of her breath. He feels in her in this moment womankind, every girl, every spark and dream, every possible future. He feels in her, truly, Harmony.

He pulls away. She says, "Be careful." Taking half of a backwards step she offers, humbly, "What goes up sometimes flies." She looks at him and smiles, but there is fear in her eyes. Day puts her fingertips to his cheek and moves in again. Without warning her other hand dives into his pants, grabbing him, pulling him and getting him. She whispers, "Let's go to the park." He grabs her arm, her waist, but does not move her hand.

Hopelessly he kisses her.

Without a sound something changes in the room, and in the tension of her body.

Day looks past him now.

Harmony stands there, her cheeks bitten in, a lock of hair in her face. She holds her own hands, down at her waist.

He comes back from Day. Going right to Harmony, he reaches for her hand, but she steps away. He looks in her eyes. Between this kiss and the prophecy he finds no words, aware that words are not needed to make it real, that nothing could make it not.

The moment is unfinished like lightning followed by silence.

She is crying, but there is confidence in her eyes even in that pain, a sense of their unbreakable love.

"Get the fuck away from me," Harmony says, venomous. She sits on the bench closest by, hiding her wet cheeks in her palms. Her hair drapes long, thick and black through her fingers.

He goes then, toward the large glass door. He still wears his casual black clothes.

Standing still, Day says quietly, "It's not his fault. I'm relentless." Harmony sits upright, looking past her.

"He . . ." Day hesitates, glancing after Orion, at the empty glass door, before choosing not to say anything more.

After she has left the room Harmony finishes for her, to herself, "He wants it all."

The Oracle of Decision

Day pulls a goggled headset from her thick armrest. Settling this on her nose, she looks out over the arena. The bleachers' arched shape allows for an unobstructed view, even in the high seats. A tremendous clear wall encircles the arena, laced around with super-transparent, honeycombed energy dampeners. Day can see clear to the other side, more than a hundred yards. Magnifying the view through her goggles, with just a thought, she can make out faces and details in the crowd, down to a nose ring. Her eyes drift across the freak show, humans and genex, but her mind is quiet, waiting intensely. Music is beating.

With the rhythm, coming steady, her view lands on the two giant robots, battling to death in the arena. The larger one is over fifty feet tall. Day recognizes it, called Marksman. It is humanoid, a phthalo blue skeleton with four arms. Thick black dreadlocks, with glowing white stars painted on them, swing around its head. Fangs and eyes are painted on its flat face. The machine is fierce, armed with an electric katana, a long spear slung over its back, and two automatic handguns in its curved, blue, electrified grips. Day leans forward, turning a dial on her headset. Now she sees through cameras in Marksman's eyes, the other robot. Red type in the display reads its name: Kami. Statistics roll across her view, showing its win to loss ratio and vitals. Highlights fill her in on their hardware in real time.

Kami is hooded, forty-five feet tall, with an orange cape that moves behind, circling in toward her. Fuel drips from its open jaw, sharp. She has three green eyes. It moves with humanoid legs, feminine but jointed backward, and two bladed hands are seen. Further shapes shift at her back, dark.

A quick burst of gunfire does little as magnetic armor pulses, sending metal projectiles drilling into the wall. Holding two arms up as shields, Marksman steps in, unloading more self-propelled bullets, tearing through her hood with a spray of steel. Her pulse armor fires again, knocking him backward. Day switches the view to a radial third person, this time with just a thought. Lunging back twenty feet, Kami unfolds huge yellow wings. Marksman strides forward at the same moment, a quick but precise form keeping his sword ready. His dark dreadlocks swing. With a stuttered, purposeful step, Marksman readies his electrified blade and drives it squarely into her dark body, twisting and slicing upward, rending. The girls on both sides of Day scream.

"Santa mierda!" cries a voice in the sky. "That'll be the end for our challenger from the east! What a show. Let's give it up for the still-reigning champ! The Marksman V9 flatout rules middle-weight PTM3A. Keep your head on!"

His dark dreadlocks glitter. His painted, slitted eyes give no emotion. Now his power is cut and his lights dim to black. Smaller machines move around the scene, clearing debris. The arena for the Team Laser Assault begins to self-assemble before he exits. Mirrors, risers and walls come out of the floor.

The announcer appears on the massive vid-screens, his collared suit made half of see-through plastic. "Well, not a bad show but it's still going to be a couple of minutes before the TLA Tournament begins. Stick around, citizens."

Day shakes, thirsting for some sort of mellowing. She laughs, hysterically, quietly breathing out. She mutters, "Don't be a tourist."

The audience is hungry, booming above him. Orion stands in the dark, in the cluster of his team, on a large round platform elevator. Strobes flash overhead. In the darkness he put on a spare set of SLRs, strapping them over his civilian clothes at his wrists and ankles. The belt and shoulder strap holster his weapons. He snaps the buckle of his modded helmet under his chin now, flips the visor down. There are nearly as many hypothetical deaths in the TLA as in highway traffic, he thinks, and nobody dies on the road.

Slowly they rise toward the light. Tiny helicopters whir over their heads; cameras throwing closeups to all the screens, including the giant ones high above. The upper stories of the maze-like battlefield shine—bunkers and turrets, catwalks and towers, a futuristic 3D terrain.

Without noise the elevator stops, still well below ground level. The players around him draw weapons. Rifles and swords come out. They all carry more. A woman nearby unhinges a long folding bo staff from her hip.

The Coliseum is dim. Glittering fog emanates from vents throughout the arena. The announcer bellows, "Are you ready for this?! For the best in live action entertainment? Witness the tricks, the wits and the shock! Are you ready for the best of Asturian TLA?" He holds his breath, then answers himself, "Yes!"

The colossal audience riots with affirmation.

Echoing via satellites, the scene is relayed to over a million live viewers, in digital waves, like a bird among the stars. Faith watches the chaos horizon, where hypotheticals and futurespace crest to become history. Events with high visibility are error-checked in real time. The Accuracy Quotient today is way lower than usual, due somewhat to her personal actions, at .99997, adjusted to minimize the effects of causal holes.

She finds herself rethinking the basic science, wrapping her mind around things her emotions refuse. The science is not that choices do not exist, but that they are nearly always predictable. People are driven by macro forces of thought, emotion and personality, and the Attractor models these. Faith has had no time to work through all of the tested possibilities. It would take lifetimes to fully comprehend the potential paths of even twenty-four hours. Yet in them all Orion, and so with Faith, refuses to believe he is not in control.

Embedded in his visor, a heads-up-display flickers on, indicating the zero score, his capture flags, the charge of his weapons and a small radar map, dense with a cluster of dots representing his team.

Cameras hover around.

TLA fashion varies by theme and modification, sexuality and style, from layered jumpsuits to oriental robes. Even without any genex in this division, the players are impressively fit. They wear shock limiters at their wrists, waist, neck and calves, and these turn on now, running with dark blue lights. The gauntlet is worn on his left arm. Orion looks at this now, selecting options manually from a holoscreen. The QB has playcalled for a seeker-heavy lineup, with two catchers. Orion selects one of the open support positions and confirms. The large light on his gauntlet engages, turning a dark violet.

A wave of something like vertigo washes over him, and he puts a hand out to steady himself on the wall. Thoughts compete for his focus.

He wonders if Harmony is watching through his lens.

What is a kiss compared to years?

One of his teammates walks past, changing position, and puts her hand on Orion's back. "Glad you made it." Then the elevator is rising again, into the noise and the light.

Each moment opens, blooming before Faith's eyes. Lasers flash through the fog. The opposing team, Marilia, is lit in red, and their seekers, with orange gauntlets, are advancing deftly between obstacles under cover fire. Orion is on the support line, and draws a bead with his anglesight around a corner. An enemy he tracks exposes herself just enough that he fires his rifle. Instantly the red limiter ring on her neck takes a hit. Shocked in the shoulder, she flinches backward. A tally light shows in his hud, Orion's capture flags rising by one. This flag is also rendered in living hologram, coming out the base of his helmet and down his back. As players gain score, their flags trail behind them, tied together in victorious tatters. His shot having given away his location, Orion immediately ducks toward the next cover, a wall of mirrors. Two members of his team spread out at the same time, in other directions. A shock grenade rolls in. It sparks at his back, a prism of color that lights the walls nearby, striking him in three places at once. The energy pulses through his limbs like tasers, nearly dropping him—his flags decrease by two, and though he staggers he does not stop, coming up a small set of stairs.

A scout on his team releases a bird—a drone—and its video comes up on Orion's screen. Two reds ascend uncontested stairs, gaining higher ground, while a third plays support below. A seeker with Halcyon is making her move across some open space ahead. Orion covers her, though he sees no opponents. He lights up the obstacles ahead of her, then pivots and steps around the next corner. TLA is like playing chess, he often thinks. While dancing. He rests his hand on the baton at his waist. Beams cut through ahead in numerous directions, but Orion hangs back. A button on his rifle creates a sonic pulse, showing two red dots on his radar display, two opponents, closing in on him from behind a wall. The pulse lights up his position with a visible flash. He pulls the pin on a decoy at his waist, palming it to a low wall as he steps across the gap to his left, away from the incoming seekers. Without pause he comes around the next opening, circling toward them. The clearing to his right now is lit, through the smoke, by an oversize hologram, a bird twice as tall as a man, raising its wings. Behind her is a tower, five stories high. It has three arms, enclosed catwalks coming off in curves toward the balconies, giving the impression of a huge tree.

Out of cover he moves fast and the two shots that trace him both miss, by slim margins, before he is around the next wall. In one motion Orion swings his rifle to his back, where it is pulled to the magnetic shoulder strap, and unsheathes his control baton. With a cracking sound it extends automatically in his grip, two feet additional. This noise is easily missed in the chaos of the arena, but the sound coming from his modded decoy is not, blaring an industrial-metal cover of the love theme from Romeo and Juliet, audible now from two walls away. His captured flags have made him a target, fluttering at his back. Orion hits his radar again. Two more reds follow him now. He cuts right, without seeing them, behind another wall. Breathing steady he holds tight to the corner. Another blue converges on his position, giving a nod in his direction. A bird zips past, red.

On both sides of them burst clouds of inky smoke, tendrils expanding, quickly filling the space. Orion's hud responds with thermal imaging, so that he sees the Marilian coming, her staff spinning in his direction, just in time to duck and counter. She is faster, avoiding him and following through with a stuttered feint toward his teammate. The two Halcyonites move in concert, swinging in on her. She dodges, blocks Orion, and then connects, fierce with his partner's chest, knocking him, stumbling back into the smoke. As she sweeps toward Orion he brings his baton down across her forearm and then forward. Orion's flag-count increases again as he tags her, fast in the abs, and the lights on her limiters go out. Meanwhile another red seeker dashes past, a kimono trailing behind, toward the Halcyon team flag.

As Orion gives chase, above him through rafters on the next level, shines a burst of emerald light, then another.

He does not hesitate—he changes direction, ducking an offensive drone. The baseball–size sphere turns too slowly, but releases a screeching sound, drawing attention. His baton retracted, it snaps onto his belt. With a movement of the wrists Orion draws his two pistols.

Heedless of the fog lighting up all around, he moves quickly from one corner to another through the maze, leaping up another small staircase to the second level. Taking cover by a low wall, he depresses levers on the handles of his guns and they unfold into discs in his hands. Orion releases these drones into the air, where they hover nearby him. The light on his gauntlet turns white, identifying his change of position from support to scout, though this is a ruse. As he comes around the next opening a beam nicks his shoulder, but it is scarcely enough to slow him down. Another shot knocks one of his drones out, sputtering into the wall. He does not stop. Coming around again into the clearing, he sees, behind the maelstrom of smoke, light and flight, the tree-like tower.

Orion. Harmony said his name like dew on a warming morning, hiking in the hills beyond Halcyon. The sun was behind her, and the wind to her side.

Day digs her fingers under the edge of her seat, watching in her headset through the camera in his visor, as he climbs the long ladder in the tower. She clenches her fists as he emerges on top, and bracing against the transparent guard-wall takes hold of the twin handles of the turret there, swinging it up and around, squeezing both triggers. Four Marilians are on the uppermost tier, sitting in a circle uncontested, in a séance formation, and Orion lays waste to them. Two floors below he can see one of the green-lit Enforcers they have summoned, clearing Orion's teammates with genex agility and speed.

Behind him the guardwall is lit by opposing fire, from another tower now claimed by the enemy.

The big man is too quick. He dashes to the side, unscathed by Orion's light, raises his cannon, but hesitates. With the next shot Orion finds his target, knocking him back. Orion's hair stands on end, as with a risen electricity in the air. Alternating barrels now he drives him back to the wall. The Enforcer almost drops his weapon. Instead he draws a line on Orion and fires.

With a loud slam a drone outside smashes into the wall behind him.

There is no significant time between the pull of the Enforcer's trigger and the impact of the light on the front of the turret.

In that second as it lurches, unnaturally, he feels a strange release, like flight, out of control. The shock travels through his fingers, through his arms to his chest. Orion cannot let go. Sparks erupt from his gloves as they melt to the handles. They do nothing to protect my love.

Harmony is watching through the large vidscreen, embedded in the glass door of the waiting room. A thick dark-skinned girl, with long white dreadlocks, stands nearby. Power is cut to the tower immediately, but this does not help him, as the pent energy releases with an explosion. She is helpless witnessing his flight, backward right through the shattering guardwall and fully into the air, his bracers flashing against his black clothes.

His body hits the dark ground, in silence. It shakes her, tremors through her. Harmony chokes, on a surge of helplessness and pain.

Glass settles. A thin line of smoke rises from his fingers.

Her next breath eventually comes, in a rasp, like fire.

From the other side of the arena Sayd watches his brother go down. Dressed in a green-circuited jumpsuit, he drops his cannon and vaults over a railing, landing with deft grace. Removing his helmet, he walks slowly to Orion's side. Kneeling, he places one hand beneath his neck, cupping his head in his palm. Leaning close, he struggles in disbelief at what is happening. He wonders if Harmony is watching through his eyes.

A slight motion touches his ear, near Orion's mouth.

Putting his large hand on Orion's neck, Sayd checks for a pulse, but cannot tell. He does not seem to breathe.

Kneeling there, he expects somehow to know if what he holds is no longer Orion. This knowledge does not come. He raises his eyes to the bleachers, all those faces, met with silence.

The Wind and the Horizon

Ghosts come like bots, their gray coats long, thin and clean. Their faces are masks, with eyes dark, like oil. A stretcher follows, automatic, as they move on the screen. Harmony trembles but she stands, her fear frozen behind open eyes. They pause beside Orion. Then they kneel. They gently lift him and place him on it. There is a moment of silence while they just stand there, and then they start to move away. The thick glass door opens quietly, breaking the illusion. She scarcely moves, just back a half step, politely.

People are coming toward her. Sayd is with them. Their eyes come together. "I," he begins to say, stopping before her. Others are moving around them now, with sweat making their downturned faces shine. Sayd steps closer, pulls her to him, and she falls into him. Speaking low at her ear his breath warms her cheek. Holding her tightly, he whispers, "Harmony . . ."

What is it? She does not open her mouth.

He breathes, "This can't be real. This isn't right."

No, Sayd.

Pushing out of his hold she looks up at his face. Her vision is blurred with such pain that she only sees in him his brother. Without his color, or his augmentation, the cheeks are the same, the lips are the same. Her lips form the words, Where'd they take him? Harmony moves past him, just a few steps into the arena and stops.

Day hurries from the bleachers but the crowd is slow, in knots. She pushes into an overfull elevator. People are whispering. A tall man on her right is covered in short dark brown fur. Spiral horns ascend from his scalp. Something in his face is equine. When the doors part Day runs, but the hall is long and wide.

Turning a corner, sighting Harmony coming forward she slows. Day looks down as she passes.

The announcer, having changed into a stark black suit, penetrates the quiet with an empty voice, “In honor of our soldado caido, the tournament will be postponed. Sonya Lei, in our audience tonight, will be taking the stage for a concert. Meanwhile Channel Xero will be airing all new developments in this,” he pauses, measured, “tragedy.” At his cue the volume begins to rise around her, people talking, moving, uncertain for just a moment and then quickly surging louder.

The sun is a silent fireball falling from the sky as Harmony comes through the gates of the Coliseum. Purple clouds gather thinly above, in its wake. People are all around, unaware of her. They move before her in an empty haze—bright as sunlight on shattered glass. Harmony shades her eyes and walks forward. A camera whizzes by above her, then another. A few people on the lawn are looking at her. Impotence shears through her heart. Her feet just go.

Time stutters and wheels around her.

Finding herself at the rail station, she boards the first car. Nearly home she pauses at a Q, gets a gray bottle of vodka, takes it with her. She rides the elevator to the top of her building. There are stairs that lead to the roof, cold. The gray door opens before her, and there is blue sky. She feels the sun pouring out again.

Azad is not there.

Alone she walks to the edge of the roof, in her black raincoat, holding her bottle in one hand. Halcyon expands around her.

Unscrewing the two pieces of the security bottle cap, from the edge of the roof she flings them with her wrist, spinning them into the air. They whistle through it and fall, separating in mid-arc, glinting orange in the late rays of sun. For a second she worries that they might hurt someone. That's impossible.

She shakes her head. She sees a sweeper way down below, a dark oval on the street. The edge, of glass, is sharp. Vertigo gives her warning, and she takes a step back, looking up at the sky.

They did not protect him. Orion, she pleads. Those assholes just took you away. What weakness. I couldn't follow. With a slow pull from the bottle poison catches dry in her throat. She removes her raincoat, dropping it at her feet. It curls around her ankles.

The wind has picked up, crawling up her shirt, over her arms, around her waist and past her face. She welcomes its cool touch. A raindrop descends from the clouds to her forehead, as a tear rolls down her cheek. Soon it will be echoed by a hundred thousand more. Right now she just kneels, staring as if hypnotized.

Despite her longing, not for a second did she think that he was done. So young. The shock that dams her eyes has no hold on the sky. From out of nowhere, thickening clouds reflect darkly in the platinum towers. A chilled undercurrent comes in on the breeze, and the ocean storm just begins to open again. Harmony shivers in the raindrops but does not move from her knees.

These games we make of life. All of the things that add no meaning. Give no warmth. We sell ourselves away. So cheap. She laughs, in love. Just fools, chasing sunshine.

Reality is a liquid thing, she feels. There is no truth. No hope. Is there even love? The future just washes away. Anything you can gain will fade. It will leave you so drained. She lies back on the hard, flat roof, staring up into the sky. The bottle tips and rolls aside, gulping air. The wind pours over her and runs through her. It says,

Come with me.

Nightfall Looms

Sayd shivers, the room getting colder now. The players around him are silent shapes in his periphery, but for a whisper. He is alone among them, unhooking buckles on his SLRs, unable to get his mind out of the arena. Violet and Scarla enter and come to him, saying nothing.

Sayd fights for concentration. He takes his coat from her gentle hand. His claustrophobic haze only intensifies. Each inhale is a struggle. Death is in the air like a shadow, dark and empty. Dropping down onto one knee, he stares at the floor, fighting to regain his breath. Repeatedly, white light in flashes throws long shadows across him. Looking up he sees a small, pig-tailed punk blonde, with a box camera training his way.

Sayd staggers toward the door, into the hall, throbbing now with people and noise. Violet and Scarla follow him, pushing into the crowd.

Day is alone, silent, feeling everything intensely. Some music is throbbing like liquid in her ears. A multitude has gathered, stressing the capacity of the hall. One fan near her jostles and shoves for position, trying to reach the door and see. When Sayd emerges, Day is pushed back against the wall. As he passes, numerous fans spill into the waiting room. They stare at the players, the flying cameras, and a few dash through the glass doors into the arena—they desire, irrationally, closeness to death.

Sayd is strangely singular, amid the masses awesome and central, passing into the brightly lit halls. Day follows.

Away from the Coliseum, as deep afternoon turns toward evening, they walk under blossoming lights. Only a few other pedestrians are seen. Two cameras quietly buzz in the air above him, keeping a steady distance. Scarla stops at a bench, but does not sit, leaning her arms on the back of it.

He turns on them. Beneath his raincoat the green circuits of his TLA jumpsuit glitter against black. The sun descends, in geometric reflections behind him, striking the glass and steel with burnt colors. Cars pass intermittently, round soft headlamps coming on.

Violet offers softly, "This isn't your fault."

Scanning around he finds that no one is watching them. No one cares to hear him. He says openly, as if testing the belief, "I felt him stop breathing, in my goddamn arms."

Scarla says, "You tried to warn him!" She smiles, "You should be satisfied with that. Guilty men are never free."

Sayd shakes his head and asks, "What?"

"For every darkness there is light, for every night, dawn. Even death can give life." Suddenly she laughs loudly, the sound cracked with loss, looking at the hard planes of glass behind him, scattering the sunset in bold polygons. Without warning she slaps him across the face, and with no remorse a second time with the same hand.

As she steps away he shoves her, with one arm, backward, hard so that she staggers. She regains her feet, silent. A skinny hand rises to her lip, bitten. A couple stops nearby, watching now. The man pulls out his phone. Cameras hover above them, cold gray against the sapphire of those windows.

Sayd moans, looking at her as he turns. He walks away. A few steps after, they follow. They come to a stop in front of a purple and black brick building. Beneath a canopy that is slinking in the breeze stand a few punks, talking and laughing. Sayd looks back at the blackness of the road, dark amid the fading sunset. He shivers with a difficult breath.

A bead of sweat stings in his eye. Halcyon is afire in changing color as the sun descends. As he stares, reality comes up to settle thickly around him. For a second he feels the unbearable truth of the night. Alone, now more than ever, we never stop and never know. This void swallows everything. "Give me peace," he mutters, speaking to no one. He thinks, Take me away again. Put me back in the hole. There is an old man, dirty, a drug fiend, bleeding on the asphalt, under the shadow of a cold moon. No, Sayd thinks, blinking, he's not here. He's not real.

In answer the purpling skies begin to fall. Quickly it is a torrent, and they enter the bar to escape the storm.

Scion Mine

Shadows heave and shake, a moving darkness cast by a bubbling light, pulsing, shifting colors to decadent beats in the bassragga dive. Girls dance in slim black cages, almost nude. The one closest to the door has a great mane of dark hair, like a river over her shoulder. People are fucking, in a deep booth near the front of the club, a group of three or four females. A large, empty bottle of X rolls sideways on their table. Laughter is wild where punks are drinking and talking through vapors. The tables are circular, with holes in the centers from which stem tall glass cylinders. Some have large display screens, aglow with art and pornography. A translucent fog moves among them all. Hombre, on the stage with a microphone, backed by his all-girl band, isn't getting enough pussy. His voice is fed through his bass guitar, deep and electronic. In the land of plenty he just lost his last penny. A few groups of longhaired dancers groove by the stage, one girl putting her arms up. An emerald plaque on the wall near the entrance reads:

Scion Mine, Asturias. Est. 2043. Freedom is power.

The revelations of the twenty-first century did not end with science, altering many facets of society to the point of rebirth. In 2041, a multinational collective of hackers, living underground and calling themselves King, took over the Strange Attractor network, exposing the entire World Database to light. The revelation was incomparable, the greatest intelligence disclosure in history, making public not simply the backroom deals and illegal actions, but the most intimate details, the raw thoughts, of leaders of industry and the world. There were Judges that were true, but many were thieves, even rapists or closeted pedophiles. They gave themselves away for past crimes by the thousands, unable to control their own fears. Government representatives around the world were nearly all liars, bankers worth billions were revealed as frauds, and presidents likewise with dictators were cons, murderers. The dethroning was violent, quick, jagger forces arresting the elite by the will of an unsatisfied world, empowered by the epic wealth of this information. These criminals among the riches crashed in a wave of suicide and convictions. Prison populations exploded. Unable to stop this, governments were subjugated with scarcely a shot fired, not to the hackers but to the people. The technocracy that rose in their stead survived by a willingness to operate without privacy. Attractor terminals were installed in public libraries around the globe, in the diamond cities, the garden utopias that were blooming—crowning the New Renaissance.

Yet it was not only the leaders that were disrobed. People in their masses were confronted with their own decadence, the Strange Attractors mapping every thought and making public their desires. There were protests, violent resistance as privacy heaved its dying breath, but these went quickly. The justice systems of the world staggered under such weight. Illegal drug use, sexual deviance and petty theft were not only common, but actually practiced in some form, at some time, by a clear majority of the population of the world. It was impossible to process so much crime. Through the Curtain Call, as the hack of King came to be known, statistical evaluation became normalized. An army of enthusiasts and hackers compiled the data, redefining expectations for the first time in accordance with the widespread human reality. Violent abuse and devious manipulation were outliers, and hence preventable with the new technology, but it was revealed dominantly in the statistics that the prevailing laws of consent and obscenity, age, ownership and substance control were not even close to representative. A new generation was coming to terms with the death of privacy, and most did not share in some morals of the old traditions, made obsolete by the revolutions of medicine and production. So came the Rules of True Intent, wiping all victimless crimes from the jaggers' jurisdiction. The cracks in the judicial halls began to spread, so wide that none would be kept in. The prisons that were filled to bursting only months before, emptied, left useless among the old concrete deserts.

Theft and most personal property law went practically obsolete well before the Curtain Call, in the feast that was the new world. Yet the vastness of the surviving black market and the omnipresence of thought-crime brought to light by King still could not be hidden.

Thus, international law was stripped to rights. Borders were dissolving, to become mere formalities. The rule of the UN Parliament was now the authority of the Strange Attractor itself, and this was natural, uncontestable, a coup of time. Those who came under its umbrella were made rich beyond money, lifted not by socialism or capitalism, as both fell away discarded, but by plenty beyond all want. The law of the technocracy was no longer a law of the ideals of powerful untouchables, lost in denial or ancient texts. It followed the awakening principals of manalight philosophy, a system of beliefs that rose in the west, emphasizing creation and the universality of soul, freedom, love and life on Earth. In this new paradigm the potential of man was set loose. This Attractor serves not money but people, in common law, in simple terms and without vengeance. The laws of Halcyon are rarely broken and often forgive, allowing for both order and liberty, both safety and freedom—allowing mankind to live and let live.

King spoke on billions of screens at once. The shock to society was irreversible. Privacy was history by 2043, when the Tally of Desires carved a path for unimagined civil freedom and honest, worldwide democracy. Yet greater than this systemic revolution was the internal, the bravery, the frightened coming of the truth out of hiding, exhibiting the soul of man. The Scion Mine gives homage to these years with an emerald plaque, bearing a populist rewording of Newton's second law of thermodynamics. As practiced by the art collective behind the clubs—anarchist, utopian and cultish—it is an axiom without exception.

Five men in gray hoodies enter under the dim lights of the bar, going to a side table.

All these blossoms of art and music unfolded in the latter years of the New Renaissance, with these gifts that created so much time, this collapse of governance and justice, scarcity economics and class sociology. Thereby the rise of a new world came in the blink of a decade.

The girl with the big dark mane, in the cage nearest the front, flickers then vanishes, a hologram. A live dancer enters via a rolling stairstep. A bare silver cross glitters against the skin beneath her collarbone. Girls step up across the room until all of the cages are full of sexually dominant, young and fit women. The next beat is hard, and they dance like fire. As the music goes on, the girl with the cross starts to masturbate, leaning back in her cage. Sex moves through the room like a ghost, table to table, in the smoke.

Minutes later Sayd comes through the door. Heads turn toward him as he walks to the back, to a vacant table where three drinks await, cleanly displayed. Taking his chair in reverse, with a sip, Sayd looks around. A camerabug whirs nearby. Noticing the five men in gray Sayd looks to the table, where Scarla and Violet have removed their coats to sit, and he says, quietly, "They are right there."

"Jags," Violet confirms. "Really, we're at a shroom club, honey. They're always here. You're in shock, love."

Recognizing them as elite ranks, cyberpaths jacked with upgrades, Sayd sees them with a mixture of fear, jealousy and distaste. They are unbreakable, genex and they are chipped, integrated and online, tricked out with adrenal boosts and simulated telepathy. Sayd is no challenge for five of them, and he knows this, so he fears them, sitting placidly, not watching him, not doing anything. He desires another beer before he consciously thinks of it, downing the rest of his first, and another is already being brought to him, on a ringed silver platter, in the slim hand of a wheeled waitress-bot.

"You're welcome," she says sarcastically, rolling away.

He turns to see the stage. Over a sweeping guitar the Witchy Sisters sing backup, "Lost spirit, take me under your wing." Purple lights shift to white with the low bass line, passing over a teenage girl near the door. Day's feathers are folded at her back as she sits drinking, looking aside when he sees her, now in the dark beneath the moving light again. From where he sits he sees her hand shake. She wears no coat and the rain has soaked her through.

Orion, he thinks, consciously settling his breath.

A dreadpunk at the next table talks loudly into his phone, "Funshow. Hold on." He pauses to suck at the blue tube in his hand, then exhaling a cloud of gray vapor which curls around, away from his face and slowly up. "I'm sure they will. How could they not, not show that on prime time? Get real, Gip. Yeah I want to see. I'm getting video now."

"Listen," says Scarla, darkly to Sayd.

The punk goes on, as the screen on his table lights up, "You're coming through. Oh that's gorgor!" He lowers his voice, "Maldita." Sayd stands. "Out of chaos, light." The screen flashes across multiple perspectives, showing a news feed about the TLA, the tower, Orion. "We are merely players." Sayd is now in front of the boy, who looks up in a daze, smiling. "What can I do for you hombre?" he says, putting out his hands, the tube and phone. His face is hollow and gray, his jaw shadowed with one dark jag of fur. One black dread of hair springs from his otherwise bald scalp. Vapor trails from three fleshy gills, in his thick neck. Looking at Sayd with a bloodshot, steady eye he says, "My boy, el chalado." Sayd sees that the punk's pants are unbuttoned. He stutters, "C-control your odor, bro-"

Sayd's voice is low and smooth, "I am not your brother." He barely starts to move and his arm is caught from behind. Then there are four sap-gloved hands on him, tearing him back and down. That fast he is pinned on the floor. They aren't wrong, he thinks, I was about to rip the kid in two. The tazer hits and Sayd loses consciousness quickly.

Day stands behind them at the door, pushing ahead of the gray-skinned dreadpunk, who is still on the phone. She is not sure what to do. The rain is cold on her soft skin as she steps into the night, and she wishes that she had not left her coat behind.

In the back of the jags' SUV, Sayd's view is fuzzy as he wakes. Gray night and lights fly by the window. Stopping, they delay a long, dark, silent time before opening the door. "Your intention was the result of temporary insanity." They lay him on the rise of the hill. "Halcyon forgives. You'll regain major motor function within an hour." Sayd is left on the grass in front of his apartment building, staring into the rain, unable even to turn his face.

Raindrops spatter on his cheeks, and over the course of minutes he begins to feel them. Cars come and then fade in the city's hum. Lights in the apartments stretching away from him stream seamlessly into the stars and clouds—rolling ominous through his vision. He thinks, Orion, was your life wasted? Just to become vile entertainment for a half-breed? What's wrong with our hearts? Did you know? It was all for nothing. The torture of your soul. He wonders what Orion must have felt as he . . . He wonders if he thought anything at all after the fall. The darkening sky has no answer, vacant.

Where is your hunter? he taunts.

As if in answer a birdwoman sweeps past, away in a long black coat, not that high above, gracefully a mysterious shape—shadowed v, trailing light and rain—and Sayd finds the strength, painfully, to close his eyes. There he sees Orion. His likeness, the blue of his eyes hangs on in defiance of time.

Day is shivering wet, watching the girls assist him across the lawn. Closing in as they reach the door she stutters then shouts, tearing up unexpectedly, “Hey! Can I come up?” Her slim body trembles. Water runs from her wings in thin rivulets.

Tomorrow's Call

This must be some mad dream, Day thinks. This is it, like it or not. It doesn't wait for me, not even now, it won't slow down. Remembering her grandfather's words she thinks, Life is a bull ride—this makes her laugh out loud, drawing strange looks from the room. She is still high from the club. Her clothes are dripping. Her eyes are getting heavily tired. Her head aches, though the pounding of her heart is quieting.

Sayd hobbles to the couch, the two ladies holding him up, and they help him down onto it. He closes his eyes. Violet kneels beside him, a hand in his hair, while Scarla seats herself in a chair nearby. Day stands shivering, dripping on the tile near the door. Violet says, "What a terrible day."

"At least we're home," Scarla coos.

Day, stepping closer, tries to shake her feathers dry.

Sayd says quietly, "The jags just brought me home." He stares at the ceiling. "I can't feel anything, Vi."

Violet rises to her feet and goes to the kitchen. Returning, bearing three shot glasses between her fingers, she asks, "Farfall, do you want one?" She pushes a smile. "If not, I get two."

Day takes the glass, tossing back the liquor immediately. She says, "Why do you call me that?" She feels the drink settle lightly into her.

The silence is a wall, but after a minute Sayd answers, "It just means mariposa."

Silence comes again.

Violet looks up, her eyes wet with unspoken tears. Then she asks, "Where are you from?"

"Cleveland," Day says. Fearing the hard quiet she divests, "I've been a foster kid. And a runaway. For years I lived with a hacker collective. But I take care of myself. Well, most days."

Violet offers plainly, with a mildly surreal smile, motioning to Scarla, "You're a long way from home. We're all orphans." The silence comes down on both sides of her words.

Day says, "Everyone is."

"Oh, well yes." Then, "How old are you?"

Day answers, "Seventeen." After a moment she laughs. "Fucking with you." Her laughter slows.

"I'll get another round," Violet announces, and soon they are drinking again. Day's world grows thicker, welcoming and warm, from within. Tucking her purple hair behind one pierced ear Violet says, "Are you just going to stand there shivering?" In a soft voice she adds, motioning to her, "Come here."

In the pearl-tiled, wide-mirrored bathroom Violet takes her slim hips with both of her hands, and smiles at her. Without asking she takes Day's shirt and brings it up. Day lifts her arms. She is wearing no bra, and her sleek body, her tight perk chest, rises with her breath. Violet helps her out of her shorts. Before she thinks of it, Violet has stripped her to her panties. The thin, pink cotton is wet through with rain. Violet tugs at the lace waistband, playfully, looking up at Day. The winged one peels them off, rolling them into a string, down the curve of her legs. Her wings clumsily bump a towel from the rack. Violet catches it in hand. She begins to dab her dry. Putting her hand on Day's thigh, she wipes away the water. The touch is very soothing, warming, and Day feels her taut muscles unclenching. She leans back into the cold tile wall, and goosebumps run down her ribs. Her naked skin shines with every touch, open, anticipating. "You're a very pretty genex," Violet whispers, and Day smiles. "Such little wings. So delicate. And very clean." Day laughs, feeling a soft kiss on her stomach. "There's nothing to be afraid of here."

Leading her by the hand into the kitchen now Violet passes her another shot, and Day laughs, hesitant, as they get drunk together. For a moment, in her naked humanity she feels alive, that even this terrible night will pass, and is only what it must be. The funeral calm, the darkness is just a shadow over the night. A genex tiger, beautiful in power and stride, the size of a retriever, comes her way. Striped in reds and deep black it approaches her cautiously, but then brushes against her skin, purring louder. Day can't shake the notion that all its lithe muscles are connected, in one flesh and one mind. With coal-pit pupils it looks up at her, stretching a menacing pink jaw, large enough to swallow her forearm whole, only yawning, sharp teeth bare and white.

"Who is this?" she asks, unsteadily.

"Ah, that's Aces. Don't be afraid. He always wants more lovin'." Violet rubs between his shoulders, and he pushes against her fingers, arcing. "He's not dangerous at all when you get to know him. Smart. Sentient you know? Just a big kitten, aintcha? Scarla still wants to castrate the poor thing, tried to do it when I was on vacation, I guess that was like ten years ago. But still fuck that!" Now something moves, a robot mouse, just a flash across the floor and he dashes after it through the doorway. They follow into the living room. Scarla is helping Sayd out of the top of his TLA suit. She looks up and caps her mouth slowly with one hand, yawning.

"Sayd," Violet says. Day is proudly aware of her nudity—genex, fit, young and angelic—as his eyes casually, easily devour her. With one hand she begins to touch herself. There is a small silver piercing, between her vaginal lips, that she rolls with her fingertip. "Leave your sorrow at the door tonight, love," Violet continues. "Tomorrow waits for none."

Now able to maintain his own balance he stands, unsteady, and walks to her, shirtless, smiling, wetness shining in his eye. Despite his bestial appearance Sayd has no body hair and very little fat. A tribal phoenix tattoo reaches over his strong chest, burning into the long fur of a stylized tiger, across his abdomen. Embers of black, tattooed fire curl intricately down his ribs, over his strong arms. "Farfall, fold your wings," he says. "Stay a while."

"Ok," says Day, quietly, with a little shrug.

Her wings do not fold, however, but open out further.

As he draws in close, Violet is standing to the side, one hand brushing up against Day's feathers. As he goes to her, she smiles, and he runs one sharp hand through her purple hair as they kiss. Stepping back, Violet pulls Day in front of her.

Sayd looks from Violet to Day. He touches her bare hip and her cheek, smiling at the blinking of her eyes. Lust curls in the gold of his iris, reflecting her light. Violet's hands are on Day's thighs, rubbing downward, holding them like small trees. Now they slide up under her arms, along her ticklish ribs and over her soft stomach. Day relaxes into Sayd as their lips meet. She feels his tongue push into her mouth. He moves slowly then, and she sucks on his lip. Violet holds her, pressing the softness of her chest between Day's shoulder blades. Reaching around she holds Day by the shoulder for a second, then coming up with the same hand softly to her cheek, turning her head to the side, breaking her from Sayd's lips and meeting her with her own. Music is playing, steady and meditative, rhythmic. Violet's other slender hand glides down over her mound and in between Day's thighs, her forearm brushing Sayd's pants, and vainly Day tries to pull back from the skin, from the fingers searching her lips. Desire is alive—pulling her—telling her that she is alive. Still she fights it as it comes, holding tight when it tries to go. It is life, like milk, pooling. For a heartbeat she thinks she is drowning. Thoughtless she moans as she releases Violet's kiss, nervously staring, into her bright eyes.

The sounds of their love are like a fire on the cold, funereal day. Wrapping one hand under her butt he lifts her. Her nude legs folded on his arm, he carries her to the bedroom. She lands gently on the big white bed. Violet unbuttons her pants, and steps out of them. Sayd walks around to the end of the mattress, watching her breathing, her ribs in the twilight, alone in the fullness of her epic youth. Scarla comes then to the door. Grabbing Day by her ankles, Sayd pulls her to him. Violet touches her hair, beside her. One kiss finds her side. In the next, Violet's lips are feeling over her small nipple. Sayd kisses her thighs, her hips, coming over her stomach below Day's belly button, prickling her skin with his stubble, and she opens her mouth, breathing heavier. Grabbing at the sheets, arcing her body a little sideways, she smiles.

"Don't stop," she says.

Your Gift

Some distant twilight paints the tunnel, deep and huge. The Prophet steps forward, her soft, bare feet rubbed blood-raw. Her pale skin, in her formal suit, is rendered slightly golden by the underground light. Her hair appears electric, white. A vision repeats in her head, of blood pooling, thickening through snow.

Something moves, like a shudder in the half-light ahead, an undefined mass, growing larger. It divides, coming quickly into dozens of forms; men and women streaked in grease, scarred and ragged, carry some mechanism of electromagnets, and belts of heavy ammunition, suddenly rushing past the lone girl in her black suit. She draws their attention, but most continue past. Three pause and look her over, walking with her. Their chatter is quiet and jagged, gutterspanish. When one speaks up, she understands only in part. "Colonial brat," the tall woman takes her hand and presses into it an old, dirty bullet. "Tell us what your prophet sees."

It takes her mind just a moment to analyze them. With great effort she opens her mouth, but no words come. Then, at first only a whisper emerges. Her few painful words, hoarse, echo in the quiet cavern with unexpected force, "You will die." More clearly, she adds, "So aim for the heart."

They disappear with the other refugees, into the dark, and quickly she is alone again beneath the conveyors. The gift drops from her red fingers, tinnily rolling away over the ageless, smooth stones.

Vast

Anesthesia does not block her vision as Harmony stares at the sky. It is not empty though her emotions would have it so. It is not sad, in epic fury. It is so alive. Stars fall through the gaps in the clouds now, as the moon shines through their tumultuous mass. They roll in the night above her, casting their drops down on her, cleansing and true, but she will not let them in. Yet they do not stop.

A slow crimson comet—a returning shuttle—descends quietly through the clouds.

What pain is in these stars? she wonders. What purpose is in that light, so alone, shining with heartache? Ridiculous bullshit of . . . us. Do they know my name? And still have nothing to say? Do they scream for Orion? Will the stars cry out, finally, if I throw myself at them? There is no answer in the vast night sky. She wonders how there could be any worth in the endlessness of nothing. Insane and brilliant, epic and vain. We're outnumbered and surrounded in the dark, tiny lights adrift—we are like snowflakes. We don't last long alone. The rain falls.

This explosion of existence. They're racing away, the stars, the planets, Orion said to her one night. Relative to us, some are moving much faster than light. Even stars, all of them will someday die.

That's depressing, she said.

It's just science, baby. Well, one way of looking, anyway. He laughed. Then, looking at the great black desert, the expanse, he said, Mortality sucks. With the confidence of one still young he added, But our limits are what define us. I never want to die. How is it ok that there was a time before I was born?

It's not rational, it's instinct, she said.

We are fleeting, Harmony. We're so fucking fragile.

She offered no further comment.

They sat together looking at the stars and shreds of cloud. His eyes brightened slightly. Well, Orion said then with a helpless grin, Maybe not though. Who promised economy to the stars? We form so many judgments about things we can barely see.

Telescopes and spectrometers—all we can say for sure is what color things are, and something of how they are moving, from here. We get really, really into our diagrams. But that's all they are, did you know? We have only hints of depth perception, realistically, until we get beyond this world. Don't you want to see it? I mean really see it around you?

She said, I think it wants us to.

I want to touch it, he answered. I want creation itself to listen to me.

She said, I want it to hear you laughing.

Orion paused, breathing. Then after a while he went on. What if the axiom is true? What if change is the only constant? Fifty years ago no one lived past one-twenty. Today it seems like this is, maybe, just a beginning. All these revolutions. I know it's easy to say but what if all of the drama, the coups and tragedies, of our coming up was just a scramble in the mud? Thirteen billion people are alive today. That's nothing compared to the number who have died! Nature does not fear death. I'll tell you that. All our fighting over money, all that darkness . . . genocide, Mao, conspiracy, climate change . . . really the mistakes of evolutionary youth, you know, kids caught up, practically, learning hopefully. I think we have no idea of the size of our reality, or of the potential of our lives.

Moments passed.

Harmony asked, Is there no afterlife?

I don't know, love.

In physics theory, even the blackest holes can give a spark. But it could be anything, really anything, out there in the dark. We claim to know. Drawing pictures of ourselves, that's mostly all what we've been doing. We've barely begun to open our eyes. In this life.

He paused, and they drifted with the night sky—a bird.

—a constellation. Imagination.

Don't forget that, Money.

Someday we might see other stars.

Silent City

There is quiet in the night. In darkness there is rest. There is a moment swallowed in the void, and the echo of a memory of falling from something less than nothing. Escape from the motion of life comes in a candle extinguished. Time breathes, and the dawn will relight. As each revolution becomes the next it becomes the last.

Azad has strong, gray eyes. At the window he stands, looking through his reflection. The hour washes away, with the rhythm of the rain. His spirit's melody flies, over blackened streets, a banshee, songbird. Deaf and down in the city, electro-cars zip by, tracing vapors of white light.

Distantly, up, the world is dark, the sky black.

Between his eyes and the glass another world turns. The streetlights pass right through.

Azad remembers a field of yellow grass, where the stems and blades were embers. They were arcs of the sun. Nature was sky-climbing trees and flutterbyes. Azad chased a grasshopper, it's long limbs shiny with dew. The boy was very small, the world huge. His father was sitting at an easel, searching slowly in the day. Azad approached him, imagination captured by the empty canvas.

He is taken from his dream when the apartment door opens and closes, and he imagines it must be Harmony with Orion. Is Day returning? he wonders. No. Hearing a stumbling in the hall he turns to see Harmony pass by his doorway alone. He hears her collapse. Going to her room he sees her, fallen graceless on top of her blanket, holding her raincoat, tightly. Her eyes are closed, her breath slow. Soaked, her black hair clings to her face.

Going to her Azad pulls her hair aside from her mouth, and removes her fingers from her raincoat, hanging it on a silver hook on the door. She does not respond, so he unties and removes both of her shoes, setting them on the floor. He retrieves the blanket from his bed, spreading it over her. She pulls the black fabric tight about her body, wearing it like a cocoon, crying, unintelligible. Sitting with his back to her bed, this moment draws long until the early morning hours, when eventually he hears her snoring and begins to relax. Azad curls up, like a bear on her floor. The rhythm of her breathing is hypnotic. It slowly coaxes him to sleep.

Harmony is flying low. They are in a warm, spring sun. Blue sky and white clouds grace her vision, vital tones bold.

She is on the ground then, resting on her back next to Orion. Grass brushes her ear, with a breeze. There is no noise but their breathing. A black kitten wanders nearby, it's fine fur glittering with galaxies. There is no rain, no rail. She smiles and sits up, watching the cat as it stands upright.

Now they are in the comfortable darkness, the Theater of Light and Sound, but Orion still holds her hand. Azad stands in the aisle, monolithic. The Theater spins galaxies, fractals, laser light behind him. Harmony is unaware of the child, embryonic, growing in her. An albatross, soaked in stars, raining deeply, sings a wordless song in the epic, galactic drama above them.

Day is flying low, whipping through the city at night. Civilization is a silver web of circling rails.

Sings the wind, It is what it'll be.

Asks the sky, How do you fly?

Desire is the current. You should try it.

How do you fly? ask the people, not looking up, raincoats shining, from the street below her. How do you fly?

She answers, You're misunderstanding gravity.

It doesn't have to hold you down.

Rise. Rise for me.

Open your eyes. Silly bastards. You are immortal.

Buildings snap past, as she fires through them, wings back.

It's easy just like walking.

Do you walk or do your legs?

Come with me. Show me the way.

And you might know wings on Earth.

Polish me.

You'll see I'm worth more than diamonds.

What am I?

She spreads her wings and feels the air, lifting her.

The distant horizon is a trumpet's call as the sun runs over.

December 31, 2051

In Vain

In the dark just before dawn, with a risen wind the downpour steadies, quick and silent at the window in Harmony's bedroom. Azad opens his eyes. She is on the bed, a shadow, snoring brokenly through the storm. The end of the night comes back to him with the citrus scent of alcohol. It's unusual, her drinking alone, thinks Azad. Then he realizes that the smell is on his hand.

He goes to the bathroom to wash them and plays a puzzle on his phone while defecating. He takes a long, hot shower. Feeling the touch of the water, in the flow of his own body, he thinks of life as a river. A waterfall. Blood is mostly water.

Entering the kitchen, he fixes cereal and a glass of light juice. When he is done the apartment is still quiet, and he stands in the vacant ambiance. The window clears at his desire. A small, wet blue bird alights on the outer windowsill, under the gray ledge, behind the autogarden, partially shrouded by carrot leaves. It eats small pellets from a feeder outside. Where have the insects gone? he wonders. After it eats Azad is still standing there. He watches it face the city and sing, muted by the glass.

Reality pulls Harmony to awareness, prickling her stubborn eyes with faint light. She fights to maintain the oblivion of her sleep—of a dream. As she opens her eyes they rest on the wall, then travel around the room, from her black TV to the digitally shuttered window, from the window to her vanity. She struggles out of her green shirt, fighting to breathe, as if the fabric were holding her to last night. The old frames on her vanity are different. Azad stands with her in the wind, stark in the sun, framed by clear blue sky and sand, fourteen years now in the past. Sayd is sitting, at sixteen his blond hair hanging past his shoulders, yellow eyes glinting in the sun, on a mossy rock before a sleek waterfall, smiling and making her laugh. The vacant frame stares. There is a brown, empty rectangle where Orion yesterday was. Sitting up her head reels, and her vision swims. A fish in a sea of oil she cannot breathe. She stands, wobbling at the knee, and rushes to the bathroom, collapsing by the toilet, where she vomits.

At the sound of his sister retching Azad comes to the door. No hangovers exist today, though he remembers them, yet she is there bent over the seat in her black bra, heaving. He quickly takes her hair behind her head, out of her face, and she looks at him.

"I can't," she stammers, unable to complete the sentence, again vomiting. Water splashes back, sprit on her lips. Harmony heaves, aching for long minutes, drying, spitting, sweating. Her vision is unreal, her lover falling from the tower, burning. Her sole desire is this purge.

Aces is on the floor, in the deep shag rug. The robot mouse is torn headless, leaving a trail of fur and wire near where he sleeps. Sayd is barefoot in boxers and loose jeans, with his back to the closet. Their skin is no less than metaphor, he thinks, it's an expression directly of so many things that I feel. Nude but for jewels, Scarla and Violet lay with the angel. Long, their uncovered forms intertwine, breathing, slowly syncopating time, asleep. Beautiful, they curve like the tension of water. Temporarily I was insane. A rapping comes at the front door, but it does not move them. Sayd goes.

Faith stands in the hallway in her light blue raincoat, drips tapping on the floor. The ends of her dark locks are heavy with rain. Looking in his eyes she says, "I've been served with an Invictus." Her voice quiets, and she looks away. "I no longer work for the Iris."

His eyes narrow. "They fired you."

"Just listen." Faith looks back to him, impatient. "It's procedural, entirely. They didn't have a choice." She brings an envelope from within her coat, gives it to him. "You never answer your emails." Her lips offer no sign of emotion. Her brown eyes are darker, deeply lined. She blinks them now, slowly. "They'll give me work though, practically anywhere but here. The future is . . . mine." She waits for him to speak but he does not. "They haven't served yours yet? Ninety-five to five they will. When they do, take the branch."

He says, "I don't work for them."

She shrugs, looking away. "Judge Pearl hates wasted lives. Here in Halcyon that is. They want me to get counseling. You were arrested last night?" She shakes her head. She laughs dryly. "You do know they could've just pulled your circuit? She's watching you. Feel free to contact her yourself. Anyway I just came by to give you that." Faith says nothing more, then turning away. She disappears into the elevator that is waiting. A veiled form, colored as a shard of the sky, she steps into the gray.

He closes the door and turns back to his apartment, returning slowly to the bedroom. Holding the envelope he looks it over, uncertain, but it is blank on the outside. He tosses it onto the end table. Day's naked, young arms hold to the white blanket, as if it were dreams—the light of oblivion. Somehow this change brings new blood to his heart. Branch? He thinks. She lies. There is no evidence against me. An Invictus detailing specific likelihoods of crimes she would commit. Interesting. No doubt info breaches. She'll go. Not me. I don't lose control.

I could do prison again, if that's my hand, but there's no Invictus here. What's in that envelope? She's right, if I was a risk, they'd just activate my felon chip.

I'll survive, but I won't leave Halcyon no matter what they say. This valley is my home, my breath, every beat of my heart—she is the only part of me that ever was free. I can't leave her to run from this. Orion wouldn't. This final thought hits him so that he turns away from the bedroom, pulls his black raincoat over his shoulders and walks out into the hallway.

Harmony will need me, he thinks. She is why he must go on. If only in his last free breath, he must see her. Too dramatic, fool, he thinks. There is nothing here worthy of what I feel. This surreal change. . . On the rail a tall bronze man in a white coat watches him. He meets the soft blue eyes with darkness in his own. The tall man looks away. A woman rides with them, sitting on the gray seats, watching the floor as Sayd sees her. Her slim legs extend in black tights from a green coat. He laughs, alone and under his breath. I could do anything. Thank god the Attractor knows the difference between thought and intention. He mutters, quoting to himself, "Our strange attraction to the fire." Everything is slipping away. Hold on to that other five. Emerging from the train he walks down the cold, wet street alone, beneath the skyscraping residential towers in the artificial light of the clouded day. A taxi pulls up beside him. Sayd hesitates but walks on.

Harmony's voice is barely there, saying, "Azad, would you go and get some painkillers for me?"

It seems too short of a time after she hears him close the front door that a knock comes. Harmony kneels still through the second raps, but the third set pulls her to her feet. She rinses her mouth. She runs water over her face.

Standing in the hall, his black raincoat dripping on the floor, Sayd's face is pale. He entreats her, "Let me in." She is silent, and somehow not surprised to see him there. He says, "I'm here. I need you to know that I'm here."

"It's not about you, Sayd," she says, still holding the door with one hand.

He hesitates, then, "We have to let go of this grudge."

"It's not about us."

"He wouldn't listen to me."

Swaying back a little, white as dust, she says emptily, without looking at him, "Every moment is a sacrifice. Anyway. We'll always have the memories, right? We'll always have history. Nothing . . . satisfies. That's all we are. Faded dust in a cracked hourglass. Lost to the wind. Time . . . sucks babe. Oh fuck." Her voice is scarcely audible, trailing off.

His demeanor breaks at the sight of her pain, but he struggles with words. "Can I just come in?"

Rising on her toes she kisses him on the cheek. "What the fuck are we supposed to do?" She leans into him, remembering in a heartbeat, something of the decades of their rambling lives. Sayd as a young man was destined to be free, not caged in these apartments.

He dreamt. Of changing the world. Owning a house, to have land like her father. The boy became a man of uncompromised emotion. Sayd was made to ride horses, she thought. He was loyal, to a fault, yet made to love all of the girls in the world.

They dreamed rich dreams sometimes together, of owning an orphanage in the valleys of Asturias.

Sayd saw a different way in life than other people, a connection to beauty, unseparated, alive.

"What of the flowers?" he asked once, on their cliff.

Distance flew off from there, a falcon with wings wide as the earth. Verdant, rolling, the span of the valleys went on. Structures rose, scattered through the woods, part of the earth. Mountainous sentinels held dark green against the graying sky. "Don't kid. I'm deadly serious. What of the bears? Somiedo? Where'll the foxes go? All of this soul? If it were up to me. To judge mankind? I'd have less mercy."

There was sorrow like rain in his words but wrath also, she knew. Harmony sometimes felt that Sayd was the Earth, in spirit, that wolf of old Asturias.

When she pulls away a tear is left behind, smeared on his cheek. Azad is standing behind him. Were it anyone else she might have started, but somehow she felt him before she opened her eyes. Azad moves past her easily, and she looks Sayd briefly in the eye before going to close the door. He puts a hand out to stop her, but not with enough force to overpower her.

He knocks on the closed door, repeatedly, more heavily, but she does not answer. Moving backward to the couch she collapses gently into its plush cushions and lies motionless, only breathing.

One Voice

A chime from the wall in front of her attracts Harmony's attention. "Turn on voice recognition," she says, not moving. "Get mail." The 51-inch television illuminates before her, unveiling a looped animation of an Irish shore at sunset, grasslands tumbling off gray cliffs into the ocean, shining with verdant life, washed in wind. A message window displays in the center, with fine black type, reading:

New mail from Faith: Orion's Manifesto

Anticipation pulls her from the couch to the screen, where she stands momentarily bathed in green, blue and golden light. Harmony touches the words with her fingertip, and the file opens. She reads:

On the Theory of Unity

She stares at these words for an indefinite time, wondering what is behind them. Harmony clears her mind, discarding preconceived thoughts. Then she presses on the screen again, and the page flips. His text begins:

Twilight comes to ages as to men, as to horizons, with a lengthening of colors.

Deep in the infinite night of space a wave crest flew, a star. Hurtling through the vastness its heart was afire. The song of gravity gave it voice. One of a trillion in the endless choir of galaxies, yet it was not lost. Around it were jewels, billions of them, dark in the cosmic storm, their intricate designs dancing precise, spinning in blackness, fast in the immensity of nothing.

This racing cloud of dark matter—this fine black tapestry, spinning in an oblong disc like a great lace shawl, inside of which ring there were empty orbits cleared by planets, crowned by moons—so much more glittering darkness. The star and its vortex of castaways spiraled through time in perfectly synchronized, random harmonic rotation. Of the largest stones, the third out from the star was a strange gem, shining outside of the visible spectrum of light, a yearning orb made aware of its circumstance by the coming of self-proclaimed life.

Blessed with water and warmth, in a bath of vapors, only in detail did this ball reveal oceans and islands, monstrous cliffs and constant motion. Tattooed with strange geometry, a crystal web grew on it of roads and towers, monuments and rails, bicycles and new lights. Somehow this third planet refused equilibrium, exploding with design and ideas as if from nowhere. The light of the sun never touched an idea. This was the shadowless womb, the subtle heart of this jewel: a myriad expression of an invisible dimension—a bridge to concepts, reason and insanity, to truth and lies.

Rockets carried machines into the sky, with thrust enough to conquer gravity, with precision enough to carve a slingshot path between the planets and through the Oort cloud, past the heliopause on a lonesome, epic journey. The void opened in absolute immensity.

They found countless things in the darkness. Worlds without stars, adrift, black systems still turning, storms of gravity and lifeless, dark masses hid throughout the infinite shroud. These wandering eyes saw the invisible and the impossible. Depth perception was a revelation to the cyclopean earth—perspective. Infinity, came the binary transmissions, is much larger than we had imagined.

And they found many things in the light.

(It breaks here, it's incomplete, even changes font
—Faith)

The cosmic sphere turned, in circles in spirals, the conflux of all dimensions, around one focus. It was the center of everything, the heart of existence, the constant beginning. Untouchable, unreachable, invisible and impossible, this was the unexplained anchor of the universe; the source; the white hole, forever open;
the endless bang.

Ecosystems of strange creatures came like volcanoes—of heat and minerals, gravity and entropy. Photosynthetic vegetation graced many worlds, as a product of light and water compounds, but often things were found that bore no resemblance to anything seen or imagined, where the attempt to describe them led to the invention of new words. The majority was younger yet balanced nearly to perfection, often more crystal than organism. Five-fingered hands were, by comparison to claws, almost unique, if inevitable still, a once in trillions of trillions rarity of physics and evolution—soft and precise.

Struggle was like a fire on a shoreline, a spark that could not persist without fuel. On Earth this fuel came like rivers from these windows of creation, these echoes of multidimensional bursting, these fountainheads of imagination—these souls. The great emptiness of space, the near infinity of unknown matter in the dark, was a canvas. Love rippled through it, in the fabric, coming from some worlds like heat from volcanoes, or light from stars.

The oddity of the Earthstone was not fully in the organization of the gases in the atmosphere, or the ceaseless activity and reproduction of the objects stuck to it. It was the statues, books and movies, the music, language and math, the intent—the freedom. It was hope built of fear, prejudice feeding ambition, fueling change. Not raw chaos, but entropy risen to live by intention. It was a will to meet the future. Awareness was, each a node in the space and time of thought. If math was a rendition of the informational components of inanimate existence, language was the more complex expression of the animated. Imagination was itself a weapon and a heart, a very counterpart to space and time.

It cried out, a psychic wave, changing the shape of the universe.

One cell formed as a perfect liquid crystal, a perpetual spark, in a cave or puddle under the sun. Through division it multiplied. It spread through the water and was washed ashore. Touching the earth, it reacted in a trillion unique ways, opening eyes, opening minds. Often it flew. Only pieces of it ever died. It evolved immunity to disease and near immortality. As they came to awareness most of its parts functioned like perfect machines, though aimless, quickly atrophying, cycling, evolving. In terrestrial boredom they still insist on an illusion of being the penultimate life.

In the darkness of the infinite nothing, we are significant. We are rare.

We are shining in the twilight of our infancy.

(Send you more soon, Harmony. I don't have the energy to convert it all tonight. There are 73 pages. I know he would want you to see it. —Faith)

Harmony steps back from the screen, her mind captured in this vision of galactic dust and alien life. Suddenly Orion is there again, talking to her. She smiles. "The twilight of our infancy," she repeats, and the monitor fades to a gentle golden shade. "Turn off voice recognition," she says. Pieces of it died, Orion says the words in her mind. She wishes he had told her more, where it was going. Though the image is thinly veiled his last thought is unfinished.

She walks to the window. With a thought it clears completely, revealing the storming day. Harmony does not smile, but her eyes lighten as they take in the dark sky.

Ocean Storm

When I see the water falling, flowing over and through everything, it confirms something we have known subconsciously all along, that the world itself is a river and gravity has us all, destined for the ocean.

She pulls her coat over yesterday's clothes and walks into the downpour, though it is less now. As the morning warms gaps open in the gray-clouded sky. The wet air moves with a cool breeze against the skin of her cheeks. Always it rains, this solemn storm. For years it comes down, weeping sulfuric over the tragedy of the Earth. Was this your plan, Dad? she thinks. You know it overran rivers and opened lakes when the ocean heaved. Whole cities met atlantean fates as dams failed and the water rushed forth. As if within the glaciers were every sin of man, their dissolution brought reckoning. Even the scientists, activists and environmentalists were unprepared for the catastrophes of the twenty-first century. The water never stopped. Nuclear dawn set fire to the seas and refugee nations burned. Rivers ran with the bodies of the poor.

Now plants and machines clean the skies, but still there is so much. The Earth is turning. The atmosphere is huge and resilient. Mankind survives, rising even still, along for the ride. I thought we might choke, she remembers. Change is inevitable, like a wave it answers only to gravity. Time doesn't notice my pain, it hardly winces at genocide—a stone on the tide. I'm but a firefly in the wind. 'Swim' is all it says.

Some eulogy for men . . .

She holds one hand to her side, feeling a crack in her ribs. I think this might be when I lose my mind. You were my light, Orion, in this broken world. Migrants came in rags to the renaissance cities. Science was a star in the vastness of our mistakes. Of course there was no plan, Dad. I know. The world is blind as we tumble through the dark. In this year, so long since that rapture, death is impossible. It was. Yet something in us is still broken. Will it always be? We don't even know what it is. The wind moves, and she wonders desperately if angels could ever truly live, behind the cold sky.

It wasn't simply men that died, when Atlas heaved. Superstition and greed met consequence head on, so that only science was left standing. There was a rift in this that Harmony felt perpetually in the middle of. There are few answers yet, in all our books, she would think, but I know that god is in these trees. I feel it. There is awareness in the universe, if there is awareness in me. Whatever it is that the soul is made of, emotions and ideas, passion and love, it could be recycled, like the body. Is intention, like atoms, immortal?

Pain's a waste, she pleads now, fighting to just breathe as she walks through the rain, pulling her black hood down. Orion is in the clouds playing vids, in a fellatio orgy with Siddhartha and a dozen pretty girls. Harmony almost laughs for a second, but she cannot let it out, for tears hang on its end.

The world has too many.

Too many dreams in this river.

There's no escaping that he has no problems now, superstitions of purgatory notwithstanding. Orion has no fear and no end. Does he have everything—anything? He doesn't have me. Gazing up at the sky she cannot even imagine a jeweled city in the darkness of those celestial currents.

So much death, she thinks. So many. So many. So many have died. So many have slept through life. Too much pain. What is it to you? She wishes god could feel her pain—like a flood, rushing from her every pore, from her eyes, filling her throat. It's not enough. I don't have that many tears. The rain quickens.

Electrocars swim past.

The Integration Complex is unsympathetic, white, low and wide, on a great golden hill rising into the mountains, at the edge of the industrial sector of Halcyon. Harmony has never been there before, and she is the only one there now. At her back, on the path, the city softly shines. A gold light, in the shape of a bare cross, glows over the black glass door. A gentle voice grants her passage, "What's lived is not undone." Inside, lights come on to guide her. Perfectly silent, they ignite along a rail ahead, and stealthily fade when she has passed. She is the only life in the windowless halls, and so now steps softly, passing closed doors.

Coming beneath an archway and through a tinted automatic door, she enters a rounded chamber. It is a large, empty, silver-blue oval, and there she finds him, alone. He rests before her on a plain steel stretcher, pale, uncovered in his casual clothes. Even now he looks strong. For a second she expects him to breathe.

The body does not move.

Approaching his side, she slows her pace, able to see fine details in his ashen cheek. A tremor runs through her as she reaches for his hand. It is blackened and cold, and she jerks away at the first touch. Staring at the tubes running from his wrists, she wonders what they are filling him with. As she continues to waver an image flickers through her brain of their most recent night together. His arms on the bed beside her were strong; he was in her body, filling her. Unable to tear her eyes from his vacant face, his apathetically straight mouth, she aches to scream.

She backs away from the empty form, turns, and hastily flees the silent violence of his oppressive, sterile tomb. The light glows ahead of her down the hall.

The Broken Ring Shines

Overwelling with anger and sorrow then she comes to his door. Her father answers and the sharpest ends of these emotions numb for a second, with one look from his wise gray eyes, one grin touching his hard cheeks.

"Come in," he says steadily. She is aware of him seeing her red eyes, her dry tears, immediately. Closing the door behind her, he hugs her to his chest and she clings to him. A full minute passes and she does not release him, burying her head in his strength, too spent to cry any more. He pushes her gently away. Stepping back, he looks at her longer, as she looks up at him. He is ancient to her, though his hair is not gray, but black as it ever was, and though his face is lined there still survives his youth. Now his clear, gentle eyes narrow. "Your heart gives you away."

"Dad!" she chokes, her stung eyes wet again.

"Take off your coat," he says, walking to the sofa. She sits, and he does too, next to her.

She wipes at her eyes, summoning the will to speak her mind. She says, "Orion was in an accident. He fell. In the TLA. I went to see his body."

His eyes go distant. "I'm sorry," he eventually says, in his voice aware of the lacking comfort in his words. He puts his arms around her again, and she rests, shaking against him.

"It's horrible," she breathes.

"Yes."

"It's my fault."

"No, love. That's not true."

Softly he strokes her hair, just once, and she thinks, Father I love you. Don't ever fucking leave me. When she pulls back from him she stares at the wall, where there is no television, only humble paintings from his brush, landscapes from his mind and from her childhood, a portrait of her face, and one of her brother. She wonders what has become of Azad. I didn't tell him where I was going. "How is this possible?" she asks quietly, wiping her eyes with one hand, curling back her lip.

Her father says, "People are so afraid. Of the unknown. Of not mattering. I'm sorry. I've no words to fix this. We're so afraid of feeling. Human. Out of control." He pauses frequently as he speaks, then goes on, his voice deep, angry and shaken. "Of our own potential." As she continues to stare at the wall, he says out loud, in a whisper, "The broken ring shines."

"Yes I know. Mana."

They sit in silence. He touches her hand. When he speaks it is deeply, "Our barbarous rules. How can there be so many revolutions in one world, and still we live and die. Exceptions." She winces at the word, and he says, "Martyr our frustration. What is the Iris, in the hands of fools?"

She laughs just a little through tears, familiarity in her words, "No riddles, Dad."

"Ok. But the Iris is a lie. So much of it."

"Science saved the world."

"Don't forget that there are whole nations still outside of our paradigm."

She focuses, "But it has fed the whole world. Cured us. Stabilized us. And in time it will build them up too. There's no denying that it knows our future."

He responds with, "Two days. We sieves of time. I guess I've learned in my life that time is visceral. Life is more than numbers. Even so much more."

She says, "The Attractor error-corrects. It knows what you imagine."

"So it can tell me why your mother's on the beach, chanting under the moon? Why do I love her? Ok it knows what I think. But what about what I know? The totality of our existence is so much more. The totality of why. Why does your brother have no shame?" They are silent. On his couch is an afghan blanket. The fabric under her fingers, for a moment makes her think of the couch in their old house, when they were younger, the real Asturian stitches drawn by the hand of Mrs. King.

Harmony sighs, laughing despite herself, saying, "Except that memory is molecular, you know. But anyway Azad's lack of humility could hardly be more natural. It's probably stranger that we do. Have shame."

"We put our faith in the machine."

Long seconds pass. She looks at the floor, pleading in her eyes. "This world can bite me, Dad. Fuck it. Truly. It can't be all there is, right? Fools thrive here. Everywhere. Orion is," she seems to choose a different word, "gone."

His voice is old, but strong, "We are all fools."

"Damn it, Dad! Fuck this!" she yells at him, and he flinches. Her tone softens, "Orion . . . Parliament doesn't have all the answers. Nobody does. Sometimes we don't add up."

"It's true."

"No. I know. I don't mean to yell at you."

"Yell. Please anything. I can see it in your eyes. I can feel it in my own throat. I'm sorry, my love. I'm sorry for putting you through the pain of this sad world.

We're all orphans. I can't fix it." After a second he says, "But I've learned from it. Our mistakes are only evidence of our innocence. Blind kids in a blizzard, are we."

She attacks him with her voice, "Well why is he gone?"

"Words are so empty, you know. Sometimes."

"Pretty clearly there's nothing, Dad." She adds, desperate, "I don't care anymore. There's no meaning in death."

He draws in a breath. Though his voice remains soft it still carries darkness and sarcasm of his own, "Everything is perspective, right? That's what your generation says. We need meaning so badly, we invent it at every turn, don't we?" He speaks slowly, "I mean all the money and contests. Well the borders, nations, our favorite stories, our crimes and punishments. Friends. Philosophy. Sacrifice, cowardice, we name it, kill or die, but even that won't . . . just make it real. Make us real. Our great, existential frustration is hardly soothed by technology either. We chase the questions of how . . ." He sighs. "Some things, some things are relatively absolute baby, among us. There are some truths that all people share, by virtue of being human. Like fragility." He hesitates, then puts his hand over hers. "Confusion. And meaning, Kiddo. Anyway. Really it is a simple and beautiful thing," he adds, touching her face, "I learned. Raising you."

She smiles unwillingly and pulls her eyes away from his. "Whatever."

"Love is the will of creation. There is no other call, in my life, than this. Life is growth. Life is love. Love is the will of creation. The meaning of my life is to create and to witness creation."

"That's manalight," she says, dismissively, wiping again at her eyes.

"We try," he answers, his own reddened now. They are quiet for a while, and Harmony listens to the music playing in the next room. It is a spare, deep piano piece, with a style as familiar to her as the stitches of that old afghan, reminiscent of the bend of the willow tree on his rolling land. He answers just before she asks, "It's one of mine."

"Sad," she comments.

"Yes," he says.

"That doesn't explain this hell?" she asks painfully. There is a note a self-reflective irony in her voice, followed by shame. Anger comes, clawing up again. "You just sidestep. There is no meaning in death. As if, if there were it doesn't fucking help."

"Death is," he pauses, "small compared to life." He smiles painfully. "When I paint a picture I destroy the canvas. When I play a song I destroy the silence. When I conceived of you, I killed my apathy. Destruction is a consequence of creation, Harmony. Every moment is a reinvention of all that came before." He pauses sadly. "You and Azad are my hope. But you are here to take my place. Life is strange. It is much more than we have imagined. We have to move forward and learn. Trust god only to be herself. But love her like you love your mother." He smiles. "Her stories are our release."

Harmony says, seriously, "You know I hate mom. Anyway, mana's just yin yang, last century shit, with salt. Don't tell me to vibrate, dad, it's nonsense. How many times do I have to beg you to come out of your books? Yes I believe in god? No, I won't worship a crucifix. But no, duality is not the only truth either. That doesn't solve it. Enlightenment by elimination. You don't break a canvas by giving it color! Orion's death is not a canvas anyway, that much I know. It isn't a sacrifice, not a counterpoint. His life was an arrow. His soul was art."

Pain comes again in his voice, tempered by the depth of his aged heart. "All of our tragedies are shadows to the laughter of god. Existence is ecstasy. In all of our pain."

She smiles at him, through her hair. Another tear falls. She mumbles, "The story isn't supposed to go like this."

"It is a message to the future, about this, this moment. But more than just the now. The movement. The shift. All of these scientific revolutions will be stillborn without the accompanying societal change, without the opening minds, the blooming hearts. We can't spread our wings without leaving our cocoon. We've been waiting, crying and dying all this time, but it's us, we are what we've been waiting for. We are the difference. If we choose to be." He says it pure and strange. She closes her eyes. Then when she opens them again he looks so sad. A minute unwinds. He says, as though to fill the silence, "I've come to believe the axiom that we truly are one soul, because I see myself in your eyes. We feed ourselves when we feed the world. You are a perfectly unique shard of universal light, my child." He takes a deep breath and goes on, "Death is . . . every moment is dying to be born. A setting sun is always at the same time rising. Face west and it is falling, face east and it is rising. In truth it's only the crest of a wave. We are like that, on the ocean of soul."

Looking at him a little incredulously, she says, "I just don't want Orion to be gone."

Somber, he says, "Fear, these westward eyes. The womb of hope." He laughs, an unexpected release, at the irony of words. He tries to gather himself but the words suffocate on emotion. Breathing out again, then he says, "Acceptance is the end of suffering, but not of sadness. Only time will ever soothe your tears. This river. Only time will let it flow. It's our decision, every moment we must let go. We must endure." She doesn't answer him. He stands, bracing a hand on her knee, and walks from the room. Returning with two glasses of ice water, he says, "The rain mourns, like god herself, for our collective soul, and it overwells. We will rise again in time. Polarity is a circle, Buddha knows, but life is an arrow, as you say. So we break through the ring. Shine through the cracks. This is mana. This is life, not merely the balance of the dao but the purposeful imbalance of feet in step, of eyes opened. Balance in motion. Those years you shared are worth more than it could ever cost. Love is worth suffering for, that's what I'm saying. His life, your past, will not fade."

"So much wasted time," she replies. "He kissed another girl yesterday. You know? God damn we are fools, you got that one right. And thank you. I can't even process it. But you really do help me. I'd be lost without you. I was ready to abandon him for it. Completely. Truly. God, I'd let him kiss anyone. I mean really he should have kissed everyone. Just let him come home. To me." Tears are running from her eyes. She stands and walks to the far wall. Her slim fingers trace over a painted portrait, her seven-year-old eyes, cheeks and smiling lips; oil colors unbroken by time. "This song of yours . . . Orion said that music is a force of nature." He nods his head. They are silent while she thinks, and now she looks toward him again. "How do you do it, Dad? How do you keep from going insane? Without hating this fucking world? Without letting it make you old?"

"I would never claim sanity." He smiles as he says this, and now again it fades. "But we are immortal. What is insanity? What is truth?"

"Truth is what you can't deny."

"It is exactly that, angel," he says, proudly. "Truth is just rhythm. It's what returns. It's there when you look again. Truth shines." He sips his water.

"You're not answering me," Harmony says.

"Sorry. I forgot there was a question," he says.

"Oh man." She wipes her face with her palms.

The rain slows to occasional drops at the window, and the sun breaks through, recasting the shadows of his face. "We exist at a confluence of dimensions of possibility, Harmony, where thought and feeling meet with time and space. Like rivers colliding. Our souls are divided. Instinct and intelligence, the artist and scientist, our body and mind tear us apart and we flow through them, like light. Our souls are like prisms, refracting the light of creation, harmonic change . . . Our burden is that we must try to understand, to focus, and this is our power. We must be willing both to define the truth and to stand away, just let it shine." Harmony is quiet. "Knowing is not in words. Focus and you'll see the key, like an eye, like an opening seed. The single constant impulse of the cosmos, the only ever-present truth, is melody, change itself, spontaneous evolution, turning nothing into something, and returning."

It is a moment after he finishes before she looks up at him. Meeting his eye she laughs mercilessly then says, though it comes out strained, dry, "Why?"

He smiles widely, happy that she is poking fun at him. "Saying a word is not the same as framing a question, my love." He coughs. "Are you asking for the cause of causation, or just trying to poke a hole in my heart? Why is self-evident. It's not words. Why is you. Why is Orion. All of these forces, in balance, in motion, are one. Symmetry, rising of itself, crystalline, long and reproductive, is like a cross, an ankh or a sword. This is life. In these ways and more we all are one."

"So, everyone should be an artist then. Everyone can be a philosopher. A billion different truths."

"Yes." He smiles, though the lines of his eyes remain heavy. "Dance. Make music, and you fulfill the promise of life. You can't escape the truth, no matter what you call it. Everything we do is creative. Everything is love. Be a beanstalk if you like, you'll still be an artist. Right now we're creating conversation."

She exhales long. Then, smiling, "I give up, Dad."

"No, you don't. Give in. You'll change the world. Revolutions are coming, it's true, even more, more than we could imagine. It's like a revelation when you get it! If you could see through my eyes . . . thank god we don't need your slavery, kid, like they did mine, or grandpa's. You have no clue how tragic it used to be just to survive, even generations ago! But they will need your gifts, I promise you. Maybe now more than ever." He talks slowly, gesturing with both hands, quietly. "What we are at its core will not change. Attractors don't understand. Because there's so much inherent inside of us, deep. We rise like a wave, reproducing our DNA, we crest, and we fall. We fly. We are true. So we must find a way to deal. What life does is grow. Very few things are totally impossible." He pauses, thinking himself clever, but catching himself. Then he says just, "Orion would get it."

Harmony is unsatisfied, saying, "Orion . . . he agreed with the science of mana thought, it's true. Nothing new. But you believe that black is white. It isn't. This pain may kill me. It's worth it. But I won't accept it! Because there's a reason." She cries openly, saying desperately, "There must be a deeper truth. I can't trust anything. I don't want to stay here." She rises and turns on him. "You don't feel this." He opens his mouth but she cuts him short, "Not like I do. It's all so damn out of balance."

He takes her hands. She sits again, visibly weak. "Sometimes I try to cover loss. With words. Be true to yourself. Trust your senses. The Earth has rhythms, and they are stable, relative to us. You may listen long to hear it beat," he says. Her eyes are cast at the floor. He adds, "You're right. Desire makes us rise. Love is life. The lens through which we focus our will."

"I don't know if I can believe it." Harmony has heard much of it before. "I don't know if it answers the question."

"Maybe I can't. Ask life, and it will answer with a tree. Death isn't made of words, child. Life isn't made of them alone. It's not only the word, love, but the breathing, rising thing. And it is fragile, eternal, like water, like we are. That's what I believe." The greater weight he gives to the words, "Forgive me if I can't do better. We echo in the air, the ocean and the stars. Forever."

"I wish he was here. I hate this life."

He answers with pause, "You don't. Darling you don't. Love is everything. It has no opposite. Love is truth. Evil—it doesn't exist. Not as a thing outside of love. You don't hate the world, its life or death, you love it so much that you're left snow-blind. You want to change it. Destroy parts of it. Create a better future. That's love, my angel. Sometimes it hurts, so often we make mistakes. We don't know which way to turn, but it is always, only, ever love that moves us."

After a silence she stands again. "I should go, Dad."

"Please don't. I don't mean to talk your ear off. Reciting platitudes."

She bends to him, hugging him tightly. "Azad is waiting for me. I don't want him to worry. I didn't tell him." She turns away.

"Harmony?" he says as she pulls on her raincoat.

"Yes?"

He speaks slowly, pausing between his sentences, "He didn't give up. He bettered our lives. Everywhere I am, he will be. What he gave you, will never die."

"I know."

As she goes to the door he stands by the couch, saying, "No one's going to live forever, despite where science will reach. But what we are together can never die." He looks heavily on her. "Every moment is a gift." She sees Azad in his face, oceanic, older, thinner. He says, and his voice stays in her mind after the words have gone, "There is freedom in life. Please remember that."

"I will, Dad. I love you," she says, blowing him a soft kiss as she used to do, when they were younger. Now she disappears into the hall outside.

Yelling at the TV

Day awakens to an empty bed. A wavy plush white blanket coils around her leg. Sol warms her bare skin, lighting on each pore, through the digital blinds. With minor pain she sits up. Her clothes are not in the bedroom, though a panty is there on the floor. She rises, stretching once, slowly, onto her toes. A shout finds her ears through the walls. She timidly cracks the door, but sensing a movement peripherally she stops. Scarla is in the big chair in the corner of the bedroom, partly hidden under a black blanket.

She looks at Day. Shifting her bare shoulders, Scarla closes her eyes. Her short red hair, scattered but tucked still at her ear, is more like fire than blood around her cheeks. Scarla opens her eyes, on Day's hip. "I love the architecture of your body."

"Thank you," she answers quietly.

"You could block out the sun." Scarla says this in a way that implies some meaning. Her arm shifts under the blanket. Day feels vulnerable, naked, as she realizes that Scarla is masturbating. Scarla's breathing quickens and her cheeks flush. Profanity comes again down the hall.

Frustrated, Scarla pushes back the blanket. She laughs then, shakenly. She pulls on the underwear and t-shirt there off the floor.

In the next room, Violet stands in front of the lit TV, watching the door. Day stays back, observing the tension.

Scarla says, walking into the room, "What's with all the yelling?"

Violet asks, "Where do you think he went?"

"Pretty obs. H-bomb."

Quietly, Violet says, "He could be at Ian's for all we know. Maybe he's with Orion? The whole thing is just fucked. But he didn't hurt anyone."

Scarla reaches the door and turns around. Her eyes catch on Day. Violet follows her look, saying casually, almost smiling at her, "Hey, lion." Day nods, lacing her arms under her breasts, holding her sides.

Scarla says, "Not lately."

Violet looks back to her, responding, "If that's what you want to bring up."

"Justice doesn't forget. Whatever."

Violet says, "What you're thinking of is revenge."

Scarla is calm. "Same diff."

Day interjects, cautious but sincere, "He didn't do anything to Orion. That was an accident."

Violet says, "She's right."

Scarla consents, crossing the room again, "If you want to know where he's going you've only got to know why, which has nothing to do with what happened and everything to do with how he feels. Come on, Momma." She looks back to the door. Sarcasm is thick in her next words, "Orion wouldn't hurt Sayd, never. He'd cut his cock right off I mean, but just for his own good. There's your damn justice, if there is such a thing. Maybe I over-dramatize, but you don't understand their history, butterfly." Despite her vocal composure her hands are shaking. She closes her eyes, standing still.

Day goes to the restroom. Sitting, naked on the cool porcelain, she pees. She shivers, stopping short. Her clothes hang on the towel rack. She puts them on though they are still damp. Squeezing her feathers through the cold wingholes, a chill runs down her back. She washes her face. Looking up, she is happy to do without the makeup on the vanity. Going back to the main room she thinks she will leave quickly. I don't want to be a part of this anymore. Nothing can be done. Off balance a moment she holds on to the wall.

As Day comes back into the room Violet is saying, "God but the bullshit we justify our existence with! Goreporn and eighties hair, you're telling me that's a career? Revenge on time, I'll say. That bitch has no sense of fairness, for sure." She laughs. "She can hardly tell beauty from plague. David or Duran Duran. The beholder is blind. Why did I waste so many lives?" The desperation in her words is visceral, though self-aware of her own nonsense, and she grins. "It's a valid fucking question. MTV. Turn off the TV." The speakers cut off suddenly and the screen goes dark. Then, "Fuck off, Kit. I'll yell at anyone I like. Don't be a jerk. I can't believe this fucking week."

Scarla sighs angrily as she lights a cigarette. She says quietly, "I'll meet you there. I always told you Harmony should have just fucked them both. No joke. That slut's pussy is gravity."

Violet says, almost laughing again but at the same time fighting sadness, sarcastic, "Really? You think he still ran to her? What the hell are we doing then?" After a deep breath she adds, "That's the problem, you know. I know you know. Yes. Love is never casual. Her time is what he wanted. Her presence. Infidelity isn't about sex. Isn't that still at the heart of it all? Are we even true to ourselves?" She takes a step but hesitates to walk away, watching the door. "All that history between them, I know. History, now time doesn't forget. Love brings the sunrise, Kitten. I get it." She smiles sadly. "No, some things can't be shared." She pauses, then, "These prisons. Our stories."

Day says, with more force than she intends, before she stops herself, "Love can be shared." The others turn to her. She looks down, more shy. "Love can."

Interrupting her, the doorknob turns and they look to it. It swings open, into the stop. Sayd comes in, dripping. His eyes shift between them, golden beneath his black hood. He stares at Day. She blushes, finding nothing adequate to say. "Morning." She rolls her wings, slowly shrugging, just breathing. Though she is clothed now she feels nude and childish, again, in his presence.

Pulling his eyes away his intensity is no less. "Get your coats, please," he says.

"Wasn't she happy to see you?" Scarla taunts, then pulling deep on her cigarette.

He answers, "She didn't have much to say."

Violet hesitates, but says, "You didn't do anything wrong my love. We're all in shock. Been going fucking crazy here without you."

He looks at her but says nothing. Turning back to the open door he throws his fist, hard, fast, slamming into the wall. With a crack the surface flexes inward. Then it pushes back, flattening, dripped with just a spot of red. He closes his eyes.

He looks sideways at Day. Standing straight she keeps his eyes. Her wings sway. "This place," he states, his voice surprisingly warm, "Come away from this place with me."

"Darling," says Violet to him, desperately frustrated.

"Fuck!" he yells at her, and she cowers at the power of his voice. Effortlessly though he calms. "I can't be here right now. I'm thinking of hitting the road. Let's go, hey?

From this whole damn city. You are welcome to come with us." He stares at Day again as he says this. Then he turns and disappears from the door, leaving them all.

Scarla's gray eyes flash beneath their lids. Jogging to the bedroom, when she comes back she emerges dressed, wearing her red raincoat and pulling into a pair of tight black pants. She gives Day half a smile and then so quickly is gone.

Violet puts on her socks and shoes by the sofa, leaving the door ajar as she leaves as well.

Alone, Day moves to the kitchen, where she finds a ripe golden apple in the autogarden on the sill. Seeing the rain resumed on the windows she shivers hard, rubbing her arms vicariously, and returns to the bedroom. She finds a dark red raincoat in the closet. An envelope catches her eye, on the end table, blank, but she only ponders it for a second. The tiger has taken over the bed, sleeping stretched among the white waves of blanket. Day watches its slow breathing, the architecture of its form.

"Take care of yourself," she says.

Moving out into the storm, she stumbles into a tall gray boy in a soaked velvet hat. Day drops her fruit, unfinished. His neck in the stiff collar of his coat bears soft, fleshy gills. "Watch it, Flyer," he says, the slits twitching as he brushes past. Standing on the curb in the rain she watches him walk away, down the road. Sayd and the girls are nowhere to be seen. Two dark-winged birdwomen glide around a corner above, at thirty feet, and cruise toward her. Almost directly overhead they split apart. One disappears from her view into the gray day behind, so she watches the other, turning her head, as she streaks out through the falling rain.

Her wings cramp under the borrowed raincoat, so she decides that she will return to Harmony's apartment, for her own.

Race the Stones

Quiet is sometimes like a storm, here streaking the windows between raindrop flows. Each rolling bead is unfinished, dragged long across the glass as the railcar ascends into the hills outside of Halcyon.

Scarla sits, her slim legs crossed beneath the trim of her coat. Violet's lavender head rests on her shoulder. Sayd stands apart from them, his feet set wide, with his hands in the pockets of his black raincoat. He gazes ahead, looking out through the beads across the window.

Harmony had hair like a deep breath of autumn night, in waves, healthy as though with the force of the rolling earth. His love for her, like a diamond did not change despite the crash of years. Sayd sees the past now in an instant all at once.

The looking glass of his decisions is clouded by regrets, and even more by doubt. Sayd came up as an orphan in the green valleys of Asturias, never knowing his parents or extended siblings until he was a teen. Unknown, the illegitimate child of one of his father's numerous lovers, Sayd was raised by two older, native Spanish parents. So he has known Harmony for longer than his birthmother, and it was a longing like a son that held him in audience to her light, through the years, swayed not by tides or revolutions, though both would rise.

When privacy died, the hackers of the Curtain Call were outed by their own devices. Some resigned in the public eye, worshipped as heroes, but as a group they were not without lies or thought-crime. Underground, they created their own Strange Attractors, fighting for independence. With these rogue SAs they killed, if in self-defense. Yet every one was rounded up by Parliament before the end. Imprisoned, caught by their own holy wars before the movement came to fruition, they were, like every other class, unprepared for the breadth of the changes coming.

The hungry, the orphans and the migrants were drawn to the Ren Cities until there was no room left even there. Population growth outpaced the renaissance construction, and population limits were drawn. They were not strictly enforced. The principles of empathy and compassion promoted by the new paradigm allowed that the flow of refugees and orphans into Halcyon would never entirely stop.

Scarla and Violet were raised in a foster home just a few miles down the old valley road from Sayd's. They met, growing up in group therapy. They were rich but mostly uneducated, sexually volatile beyond a whisper before he knew his left hand from his right. They were his friends from the beginning, growing to become his lovers then later, after his felony.

The database evolved on its own, outpacing human oversight and effective at providing for the renaissance nations as the decade came on. People found new pursuits, and new leisure, through the Curtain Call and what came after, but athletes and artists alike needed at least a sense of unpredictability for their endeavors to function. Without the burdens of money, law or war there was less fear of human overreach, so when the rules of Competitive Exception and Information Outliers were decided, Sayd and most of the world were resoundingly for them.

Remnants of King hold vigil still today above ground, hacker collectives with their own Attractors, dedicated to watching the oracles, kept clear of the Coliseum for the rule of CE.

Nothing stays the same for long.

Entropy is a force in society, Sayd knows, the predictive rule behind never ending revolution and freedom.

Like a diamond is faster than light, unchanged across any distance of time, the city is itself a storm, violent in its ambition to eclipse the stars, dark before dusk with the weather. Harmony had hopes without plans, and he fell into her like a vision yet to pass, a hawk in the wind.

Light as an Arrow

Faith has shut her eyes, knowing that whatever the future will become, it surely weighs much less than the past. There is only silence, no whirring machinery. Only her loud, beating heart interrupts the peace. Opening them again, there is nothing but blackness all around her. Forcing her thoughts into form, she thinks, habitually coding in her mind,

SEARCH[NOW ; 50392.- ; 65087.- ; G + 5'5 ; Faith]
MAP[VIS[RAI 15' ; VEC : Amber]]

There is no computer now behind my eyes, and no Prophets to answer me. Yet she knows the codes natively, thinks in their language compulsively,

NOMAP[invalid concept YGORA]
Sug[VEC : Faith] or MAP[ABS]

Holding as clear as ever in her mind, Amber in a blue dress is sitting on a park bench reading chaos theory, eating lettuce on that mustard rye in the afternoon sun. As a memory she has no coordinates, an inferred image with no mass. There is a dichotomy in the mind. When the SA mapped her awareness, they found no one sitting behind her retinas. Physics is the language in which the SA decodes thoughts, so there is no question of which comes first to the machine. Yet to the imagination, math and logic themselves are only subsets of possibility, dark, massive trees in the universal storm, roots of the Earth.

The Attractor insists that 50392 has meaning, whereas Amber is a dream. What if you're right, Orion? What if we take it further, what's the next step? If ideas are held to no absolute frame of reference? I will still miss you, Sis. Now and forever. And now our . . . little brother. Zero is zero, but you were my one.

Her innocence. There is pain. There is the soft, damp grass. And there comes a slow rain.

These bright, familiar memories bear weight now, for her soul, so often stricken by this same moment, has scarred over. I can't feel your ocean. For too many years.

I can see you. I can't touch you. I can know you. I can't hold you. How is this? Something is real—I don't know what's coming.

Again she opens her eyes, but the dark is near as her eyelids still, and Amber lingers, frail and beautiful, an invalid object in an insecure reality. Faith concentrates on her breathing. It is past noon, she thinks. Someone must come soon.

Invictus. You are forgiven, Faith. But you can no longer do your job. You are human. We are sorry for your loss.

Am I? she wondered even as she read it. What the fuck does that mean? Does forgiveness raise the dead? I am a small part of an immense machine; I accomplish things. There is no need. You can't make me human. I don't want to be . . . As she collapsed in shock into this hard chair next to her brother's empty body, in that peace, alone in the chamber, emotion surged from her subconscious, and the lights dimmed then went out. In the dark of his integration she sits, her sense of solitude diminishing. It is so out of place, she feels, their apology.

She wonders, What is going on with this power? It's only darkness. A chair. Deductive reasoning, from a single point, may render the fuller context.

Conspiracy theory is a black hole. The stuff of fools in forums who never cracked a code. It is well known, civilian Attractors are edited for the Coliseums, for the rule of Competitive Exception. These concessions for games, ink butterflies obscuring the database, potentially invalidate whole swaths of code. But they are error-checked. Occam's order holds the world together. Interpreters decide what questions to ask. Algorithms comb for pattern. Order in an entropic universe only exists because of trust.

The darkness remains.

Power does not fail in Halcyon.

Past the shadow of her shaking hands, nothing is visible in the cool chamber. If I hadn't spoken with Orion, he might still be alive. 'If' is a word without any meaning. The damn Prophets put it right in front of me. What else could they do? There is only process.

Amber does not haunt me every day. She looks straight ahead, to where she knows Orion's body is only feet away. In absolute darkness still, she sees him.

I am death's midwife.

A slow, soul-scraping sound comes, rising slowly behind her. Approaching, in the hall, it skips and tinks.

Parliament will put it right, she thinks. They see where I've been blind. My Lords do you hear me now?

Will you save me from God?

The door behind her opens. Dragging through the doorway, something crawls, agonizingly slowly, across the room, only a faint, shifting shadow. Faith thinks of running or speaking but does nothing.

Eventually a voice comes, shocking but soft, female. "Orion." It sounds immediately familiar. The voice rises unsteadily, from near where he must be. Faith does not respond, holding her breath a moment. The voice speaks quickly, "God is a satellite."

She pauses. "But I have not forgotten," she says in the darkness. There is an edge to her sound, like static. "You're right, Orion. They lack resonance fields. The earth has no ears for you. Say . . . see . . . See you later, my love." With this, something drops on the floor, sounding like a rolling coin. "Let me go. Total procrastination with this business. I am never leaving here!" She inhales loudly. "I'll finish your thought, Faith." Faith flinches in her chair, then grabbing her own hand to steady, getting to her feet. "Data cannot be self-aware. Any more than a circle can be a square. But that's just the tip." She laughs, only a single breath in the dark—it comes surprisingly easy, like a bird taking flight, then quiet returns, their breathing punctuated once by the hiss of the machinery beneath Orion.

There is a click and an explosion of light, shining brightly for half of a second. It ignites the whole chamber. The emaciated girl stands there, looking at her, in front of the body of Orion, blood crusted at her lip and sleeves. Her light hair tumbles wild around her. Then the flash dies to just a laser pointer, clear white, a perfect focused shaft in the black space, illuminating nothing, shivering. The far wall absorbs the light, not reflecting. There was blood on her hands. The girl says quietly, "Don't close your eyes."

The Prophets in Denial

Love is lost, Sayd thinks as he comes down the long hall of the SI. My soul begs only the one question. Nothing answers. Violet and Scarla walk softly behind him. A cigarette burns between his lips, loosing ashes in the air as he goes on.

The overhead lights track them, gliding, a pool surrounded by the darkness. Coming to the end of the hall, as they pass through the archway the tinted door opens ahead of them. Yet the next room remains dark. Sayd slows his step. The shadow gives way as a fresh, clear light comes on.

In her blue raincoat, Faith stands beside a black chair. It is a cheap folding kind, near the body of Orion. The atmosphere is static. As they come into the room, Faith turns her head toward them. A fizzle sounds faintly from the canister beneath Orion.

Faith's gaze returns to the girl across the room. Skinny with long, wild hair, she slouches in a rattled suit, crouched against the far wall.

Sayd stares, breathing slowly through his mouth.

Violet asks the girl, after a second, "Are you ok?"

Faith says nothing, not moving.

The girl in the suit just looks at Faith, unblinking and still, like a wild thing.

The door to the hall slides shut behind them. They hardly move through the following moments. It is Scarla who first approaches the body, and when she does it is without a word.

The girl in the suit, across the room, hums a melody, faint. Looking up at them, she says, "Did you try hard enough?"

Scarla puts up a hand between them, as though to block the words, still looking at Orion's body.

The girl runs her finger along a black crystal, about the size of a large pen. It emits a thin beam of light. Violet backs away, to the wall in a few steps, saying, "Is that a dragon? The pen. She's got a laser."

Silence passes. Only their breathing is heard.

Sayd notes how the walls are clean and smooth. The last time he was at the SI, the room they were in was entirely different from this. It had texture, decorated by family, with flowers, white lace and a large video. People were mourning. An orchestral recording played, dancing like candle-light. Somehow it all muted the stain, this overpresence, of death.

In this sterile SI room now, it is everywhere.

Asks Faith, breaking her silence in anger, "What were we supposed to do?"

The girl in the suit smiles and, pulling at her collar, she opens the knot on her blue tie, letting it come out. "The things you are blind to could block out the sun." Scarla looks her way then. The skinny girl stands, unsteadily. The light is held, nondescript in her other hand. The white laser makes a dot on the floor. "What is your decision?" Sayd watches her, frozen as she speaks. "You only get one moment, one chance to make a choice, but everything you are is in it. One life. Did you feed the world?" She pauses, and the depth of her silence extends. Her voice changes, more direct, saying, "If you knew the machine like we do. We have our own Attractors, in caves, deep underneath the Black and Mediterranean. Invisible to the Iris. Do you want to know what we saw in black holes, when the Attractor didn't know we were looking?"

Scarla interrupts, "You're a Prophet."

Faith says, "She is."

The girl seems more skeletal when standing, in her wrinkled suit, but her voice gets louder, "The Iris is the most powerful weapon ever devised. I . . ." Her voice cracks, a sound like static coming from her throat. "We are the Black Sea Uprising. We used a simple tesla destabilizer, a UEMD Ultramagnetic Coil, overloading the TLA tower from deep underground, killing Orion. To bring her here. To bring you here. And the rest is gravity." She coughs, choking. Tugging at the buttons of the shirt, near her neck, they pull open, lighting a long, skinny v of sunless, flat skin. "There's even a chance it might work, and the curtain will come tumbling down. Let the blue sky through." Pulling at the fabric harder, she rips her shirt open, untucking it in part. With that same hand she grabs at her own side, clutching herself tightly around the ribs. In the echo-less room her desperation is suddenly palpable. "The Iris has been killing since its inception. Terrorists. Thieves, hackers, pedophiles, Prophets. Somiedo. Uprisings. When were you going to start noticing? The blood at our ankles. If she had an emotion. But she'd been gone for so long. Did they set us free?" Her eyes drift, over the walls, coming to rest on Orion. She directs her words then toward him, much quieter, personal as though he had asked a question, motioning at his body. "I gave it away, ran away and it was fun at first." Her wide eyes beg. "Fuck, Baby, I was suicidal in college and you never knew. So lonely. So much like you. Nobody killed you. We're no different.

"The Iris took us, and nothing was ever the same. Every infinite corner of the world is aligned with it. You can't handle it and stay human. The truth. People are just shadows, in mirrors, breathing, speaking echoes, ignoring this epic pulse. It—it isn't even abstract. It comes in these waves that run through us—our bodies are antennas. I—I've been with you, Orion, all these years. I've been watching you. Memorizing your words before you said them. You've crossed great plains of thought since the last time we spoke. And you're right, Twilight. But readers are just . . . fleeting. So your every word was a conversation with god? Your desperation sets fire to the universe, little brother." She steps toward them, standing now near the body in her open suit, clutching her torso around, across from Scarla. Scratching, struggling, tossing her long hair forward over her shoulder, reaching at her back she seems to grab hold of something. Her tone changes again, schizophrenic and mechanical at once, "Can you see it yourself, immersed? Fool Alan. But the universe knows you're no shell. She never could completely let it go. God! She wanted to." As she says this she takes her hand out, holding a cord, connected at her back, glistening, striking her shirt with a bright dash of red. Nobody speaks. The Prophet raises her other hand, holding the light, toward Scarla. She continues looking down at the bloody, silver wire. After a minute she starts singing, slow, "Seasons don't fear the reaper."

Scarla raises her hand across the body, laying it on the pointer, gently pushing it aside, as if it were nothing. Her breathing is steady. "You're saying there was a conspiracy to kill him?"

Eyes open in shock at Scarla's hand, as though it were unnatural, the Prophet looks across the body at her, smiles widely with her thin lips and says, "Nobody is conscious of the costs." She closes her eyes. "How many names have I?" She swallows, dryly. Opening her big eyes again she says, "AI writes its own code. Headless. Murders the makers. No, no there's no conspiracy, kid. Self-preservation is a positive feedback loop. Anomaly is purged, threats to the system. Love is murder. It doesn't prove awareness! Death is meaningless. Politics is grave digging. War is endless. Who cares about shells?" she asks, desperation in her voice. "The unpunished crimes of the world don't even matter. Right? Or they would outweigh the stars." She smiles. "This pattern is huge. Death coils around the Earth. The collective is wrong. The Iris is wrong! They are the same, each trying to erase the other. Scream all you want. Think larger, microcosm. We don't matter. See the very fabric of existence is riddled with holes. Our refugee hearts. Our politics, economics and tragic, fool-blind justice—they come straight out of the sun.

"Emergent strange attractors, blameless as nature. Were you going to die for them? These undead parasites. Don't fear the Iris. You've been living with these machines for millennia.

"Attraction is destiny? That would be strange." Her lips quiver. Her words quicken, "We evolve so fast. So many chains. Keeping grounded these girls, growing wings. Will you fear them? It doesn't matter. Denial makes us blind. Mistaking sex for violence. Lust for ambition. This machine. These wings for tragedy.

"Did you feed the Earth?

"We are the generation of the reaping. We give eyes to the blind. Yet we burn the world for a dime."

Sayd moves toward her with no warning, passing Orion. In response she raises her skinny fist and the black crystal lights. The quiet explosion of the pen stops him, a shaft instantly connected with the far wall, just missing his hand. The beam ceases, doing no harm to the smooth walls of the SI. She says, "You know there is a circuit in us, Sayd? The Iris is in my fingers. There is a circuit in you. The hackers have my mind. My nervous system is just an extension of the SA." She trails off. The rest of them remain quiet. Then she says, "I haven't had an unobserved emotion in years! He's dead, and I can't cry. I'm not even angry. The future is a lifeless chain, and I can feel it on me. It didn't bring us here just to speak for the Black Sea hackers. This has already passed. The Iris has seen us all die."

Violet takes a step away from the wall, toward the door.

The Prophet is looking down at the laser, "We could sooner let go of our own hand." She blinks, pausing. "But it'll just make another one. They get wide sometimes, causative black holes . . . Nobody can see us in this well. Nothing escapes the Iris." Then, looking up at his body again, she says, "Orion, our burning angel. Bring out your Prophet, and she will lay waste to the lambs. The whole city will see. And the Iris will be laid bare, in the brutality of its cold answer, as just another . . . machine." Blinking, she looks at Sayd with no visible emotion. She whispers, "But even the Uprising doesn't get it. The Iris will crush them and the future won't notice. Until you sit with the diamond you will never grasp the interconnected oddity of the ocean you," her voice cracks, "breathe."

Faith steps forward, staring at the girl with the wild, light mane. She puts out her hand to the crystal, which rises in the other's bony grip. Despite the blood on that hand, the starvation in the Prophet's cheeks, the deep contrast of their hair, or the tear coming down Faith's face now, they reflect each other in finer details. The set of the lips, the very style of gaze, mirrors. Faith says, "I forgive you, love. Come back to me. Give me the dragon." The light cuts upward from her wrist along her arm in an instant that moves faster than pain, splitting her sleeve, cauterizing much as it twists across her collar into her neck and up again, resting on the ceiling, harmless, twitching in a beam. Small parts of Faith fall, in pieces, blue fabric and brown hair—faster than her flesh. Despite the white-hot beam, blood does come up, only slower, as her body remains standing, her last breath still moving her, staggering.

She falls.

The Prophet screams a strange, short and empty scream, tearing loose the length of wire from her spine and clawing across the air, stepping back.

Sayd comes the rest of the way at her in a stride. The Prophet swings the open laser toward him, slicing his shoulder with it before he catches her wrist. He does not flinch, though blood flies. He takes the weapon from her, pinning her to the wall with his forearm at her collar. The beam turns off. Tight-jawed he looks her over, unmoving, her big eyes in shock. Now he looks at the dragon, at Faith. Scarla steps away horrified.

The emaciated girl stutters, "Open your eyes. It has never. Even. S-s-seen you. It doesn't know you from a stone, Sayd. It owns you like a crown."

He points the crystal weapon at Orion, still holding her to the wall. "Open your eyes," he says, but his brother's body does not move.

Scarla says, clear as a knife, moving toward them, "Don't go insane." Her voice gets louder, suddenly desperate, wiping at her bleeding lip, looking wildly at the walls as though they might move. "That thing just cut her in two!" Her eyes fall on the Prophet. "Like it was nothing. Reason is your fairytale. I tell you square."

The girl answers, shaking, "No I didn't."

Scarla raises her voice at the walls. "You can't!"

Violet steps between them, "Let's go. We can get through the door. What's in those tanks. . ."

The veins in his neck strain. "Violet," he pauses. Now the dragon fires, surprising them all. Its silence reverberates through the room like a violent inhale. She crumbles to her knees, staring at him with shock, covering the hole with her hand. A lock of lavender hair obscures her eye. The dragon flashes, brightly lighting the room, and she slumps backward, her breast heaving with life. Air struggles through her, bubbling out with blood spreading on the cold steel floor. A wheezing cry strangles in Violet's throat as her body slides, and her open hands slip on the smooth floor as she tries to get up.

"No, I . . ." He blacks out.

We fall in love.

Sayd remembers the girl was crying. Terrified. Her eyes went right through him like the light of the moon. Like Harmony's. The gun made the old man a threat. The rain was in my eyes. Let it out.

I should've jumped him then. But I thought he might kill her if I did. So I waited. She was panicking. Time was passing. Raindrops. All those other people on the street didn't make a move. Her eyes showed so much emotion in that second—before I moved.

Opening his tear-stung eyes he looks over his brother's body, unsure how long he has been standing in that SI chamber. He thinks, Forgive me. Condemn me. I don't fucking care. Am I guilty? He emphasizes, I am not wise enough.

I am not innocent.

I took his gun very easily, in one motion going to him, stripping it out of his grasp—those wet fingers—and knocking him to his knees. Her foster parents were right there.

A steady trail of water moved over her cheek, luminescent in that curve, brighter somehow just then. Life and death do not spare children.

The asphalt ran with rain and their blood, but I was still breathing. Her green eyes stayed open, looking somewhere past me, warm.

Nothing changed.

Yet that changed everything.

It's what I repressed. Not shame. Revelation.

It's what I never allowed myself to see. It's the beast in my brain, the fear in my heart—the worst of all possibilities.

It's not that I killed him, my brother, my own twisted, forsaken, mirror soul, her grandfather, backed into a corner. On his knees. Not that it was too late. Useless. It's not even that it was right. If it was right.

Now the light above him in the SI winks out, dropping a blanket of darkness over the grisly room. A scarcely perceptible click and whir comes from behind him. As he turns toward it the hall is suddenly lit again, showing him the open door. Still holding the black dragon he runs from the central chamber, and the light leads him through the corridors. Bursting from the passage into the crisp air outside, he falls to his knees upon the earth, crying insensibly. A faint drizzle falls like raining glass into his open wound.

Enigma

The afternoon has grown heavy, darkened by clouds tumbling thick through the sky. Halcyon glows. Music hums through the streets, as people rise to the call of this party for their coming year. They celebrate the passing time, as they celebrate the birth of tomorrow, here in mid-winter. People are drunk, high, and some are undressed in the streets. Bots, like spiders the size of dogs, climb the buildings, decorating, hanging lights and banners. The rain has faded to a softly falling mist and the air is cooling. Something is gone. Something vital will never come again.

Entering her apartment Harmony hangs her raincoat on its hook. She sits on the couch in the living room. Taking the remote in her hand she turns on the stereo. Synthesizers moan. A diva wails. Replacing the remote on her small end table she picks up the glass pipe next to it, by her hand. The flat-screen lights up at her presence. It still bears Orion's manifesto, page three. There is so much more. We were at the beginning.

She says sadly, "Give me peace." She fakes a smile, feeling poetic, as she puts her lighter to the bowl, and it squirms alight. Slowly her lungs are filled. He's some sort of enigma, Harmony, said Orion, smiling. What? Nothing, I'm just high, shining in the twilight of my infancy, unfulfilled. Prophesizing. I'm fading.

Pulling the glass from her lips she exhales, her body shines with a moment's exhilaration, and she thinks as the cloud is rising, Put aside your fucking pipe, Lover.

Tell me what is on your mind. Nine years gone. Voice your dreams. Where is the fire? Tell me what you feel. You'll be gone tomorrow.

Share the orgasm of your brilliance with me now. Don't wait. Why are we so afraid of reality, of honestly communicating, risk, of feeling pain, of doing anything?

But I'm happy, she said to him. I couldn't be better. I can't tell you how much I love you. In our impotence there's no call for love, no room for my sadness. There's no need for me to tell you how unhappy I am, how numb I am, how I long for my youth. I don't want you to understand my pain, because it will hurt you. I'm afraid that you're not like me. I'm afraid that you might be.

Give me your hand, Orion.

I've passed through some strange dream, come out the other side, and the door sealed tight. The sky cracked and the world was made of glass. Broken by less than a kiss.

Wake up. Something is gone.

Wake up. So what if I did? And be the only one?

"Enigma," she says to her pipe, her voice shrouded in sad music. She throws the pipe hard against the wall, leaning, elbows on her knees. With a pop it broke, odd shapes of glass scattered to the floor. She crawls over to the mess and begins to pick up the pieces. A jagged one slices her index finger, giving one small bulge of blood. As she examines this drop the autoduster slips around and atomizes the pipe with hardly a sound. She desires another hit. Escape. I don't want it. Face it. I can't think as it is. It's all too much. Stop turning. Let me be true to myself. That's it. There is nothing else.

Why do we never know when we have enough?

Why are we driven by such petty fixations? We throw away our love. Why do we fail? Why do we lie?

Why does sadness turn us to such rivers, Dad?
Can forgiveness be bought?
Can mistakes be paid for?
Why is it so hard to breathe?

Going to her bedroom, she hears the crash of the shower start running. There is a crumpled raincoat on her bed. She calls, "Hello?" through the door. After a few seconds the water stops running.

The door opens and Day is there, wrapped just in Harmony's towel, brushing out the tangle of her hair. She says in a defensive tone, "I'll be leaving."

Harmony reaches past her into the sink, rinsing her hand, asking, "Where are you going?"

"I don't know. I don't think you want me here?"

"Should I?"

"It wasn't my fault."

"It doesn't fucking matter."

Her voice cracks. "Yes it does."

"Just go, Day. Get your coat and go."

"Well Orion wouldn't have touched me if you were enough. You know that's true. I slept with Sayd last night. He's your ex?"

Harmony snaps, "Get the fuck out."

Dropping the towel, Day sits on the toilet lid as she pulls on her socks. She says only, sincere but weak, "I'm sorry." Her hip is paler than her thigh, fragile. Her ribs are bows. Day's wings reflect in the bright tile, and corners of mirrors. After getting into her clothes, she moves past Harmony to the living room.

Still the stereo sings, "Be like a white dwarf star. The quicker fires fade."

Harmony follows. She looks at Day's white feathers, wet, newly cleaned, stemming from her back, from her thin shirt in two agile, living wings. Something in her light, her heedless decadence, is innocent. Curiosity. Is no sin. Putting a hand to her forehead, to block her storm of thought, Harmony says, "You're still a kid."

"What?" She turns, slowly trying to swallow. "No I'm not."

"I'm not going to waste my time hating you."

Day cries now, a tear. "I'm sorry."

"No." She thinks a moment. "Why would you be sorry? You can fly."

"No I can't." Day wipes her cheek as she says this. She takes her raincoat, moving toward the door. Looking back Day says, defiant though crying, "That's your issue, you know? You're afraid of your own emotions. Nobody needs you. Nobody gets you. Ok, well what do you want then? I've known you two days and I can tell already."

Harmony says, "I'm not hiding."

"I'm just trying to be honest." Day turns around fast and goes out.

Harmony stands still, staring at the door, for a long minute. Then she gathers her own coat and leaves the apartment.

Colored lights fall and glitter in the sky, between the towers, in the light rain of evening.

Harmony's trip uprail is quiet, as she stares, disbelieving, at the floor. It is perfectly clean.

Apparitions dance through her mind, a torrent of memory. Lifting her eyes, lights streak under the sky. The heights of the city give way to the dark hills of the Asturian wilderness.

Approaching the SI complex for the second time today, she is alone in the abnormal quiet, crossing the cold stone path, surrounded by tall, yellowed grass. Her shadow crawls away across the darkening blades.

The white building is deserted as she quietly comes to the black doors.

Watching the bare gold cross above the door, Harmony goes in. As she enters, a light appears to guide her through the branching halls.

A thrumming noise rises behind her.

Harmony stops to look back, and there is a group of bots, humming black shapes coming out of the dark. Agile robots called Artisans, tall like centaurs, humanoid torsos on curved, plated insect frames, droids taller than Harmony, their heads sleek with many sensors, look at her with green lights in their eyes. Arms are shadowy metal, at ease at their sides. Small autodusters follow them, flat rings of light in the dark. They stay near the edge of the shadow as Harmony goes on. Somewhere ahead, from the indefinite depths of the blackened tunnel, echoes some sort of dense, pounding sound. Her walk slows now, but continues toward it.

A surreal emotion wells in her, then as she crosses under the arch the tinted door opens. Coming into the darkness of the chamber, its light comes on.

Orion is there, exactly as she saw him before, but the scene has otherwise become insane. Blood pools around the bodies, the raincoats of red and sky-blue gathering. Faith is in red-streaked blue, with her mouth agape and bone showing through the split of her head. Something in the tunnel outside the room slams again. A fourth girl is near the wall, slumped and bloody in a mass of blonde and white hair, in a disheveled black and white suit. The autodusters whir past Harmony's feet.

Descending to her knees next to Faith's divided body Harmony does not know what to do. As a big insect-centaur robot comes toward her she moves away, still on her knees.

With a motion of the tinted door, Day steps into the room. She gasps, stepping back into the wall, watching in shock.

Their raincoats tear from the sticky wet floor as the droids lift the bodies of the three women.

The Artisans leave with the broken forms—the shrouds of Faith and the orphan girls—draped across their arms, walking through the doorway into the blind darkness beyond Day. One autoduster stays still, near the body of the other girl, further away. The last Artisan, like a giant insectoid stage-hand, folds and carries away the small black chair, leaving Harmony and Day alone with Orion and the motionless body of the emaciated girl with the long, light hair.

Where is Sayd? Harmony silently wonders. This is too much. It flows over her as she stands, not quite getting in.

As a minute passes, Day is drawn to the center, to where Orion rests. Viewing his sterile form, she mutters the words, "I didn't . . . I don't . . . What's in those tubes?" Turning back to Harmony she is crying, saying, "I'm going to be sick," but Harmony does not respond. Day kneels.

In a daze Harmony then goes to Orion as well. Past fear, past pain, she moves her smooth hand over his charred skin. She takes his burned palm and folds her fingers around him. Closing her eyes, she feels his hand and it brings to her being a wave, overwhelming, memories, alive and unchanged as the sky.

Harmony opens her eyes at a sound. The remaining body, the girl with the unbuttoned shirt, streaked in blood, moves.

It struggles to rise.

The hands protruding from her sleeves are thin and long-fingered, knuckles bleeding, connected to delicate wrists and forearms, scraped red. She looks up. There is a large hole clean through her forehead. Blood is dried down her face and white shirt, in her tangle of long hair.

"Harmony," she says unsteadily. Harmony does not respond. The girl speaks in quick, broken lines, a strange whine in her voice. "Day." She pauses, struggling upright. "They can't contain me." She suddenly screams, "Rion!" She jerks her head up, toward his body. "No trust. No trust. Where is your fucking trust?" The other two are motionless as she winces, apparently fighting herself, never quite looking at them. She speaks again. "I can see the future. Let me go." Now she pauses and laughs, not wiping her tear, staring up at the ceiling. "This currency of suffering. All you need is your willpower. Your birthright is this gift. Power of the sun. Love is gravity, little one. Love is gravity. Love is gravity. Crystalize. Rise. It is the only power. Stop hiding. Your bare humanity." She is agitated now, but quickly calms again, wrapping her arms around her midsection and twisting her body, saying, "Ideas like chicks hatch in blood. This is more important. That's true." She does not land her eyes squarely on her still. "Even now our mind is a database." Stepping backward into the wall she shrinks to the floor, skinny, weak and wounded. She whispers, "Thy name is greed. Machine. Thy name is legion." Harmony looks to her but the air in her is gone. The blood, in slow rivers, shines inside of her. Harmony is drawn to the sight, but afraid of the emptiness turns her eyes away.

When Harmony emerges with Day into the fresh air outside the mist is changing to light snow. The flakes are small, falling in wandering circles to the earth, slowly, gently to the grass, melting on the asphalt and steel. An explosion rings somewhere nearby. They turn their heads to see, but the snow and the hill rising steep behind the complex blind their vision. The echo comes again. They move toward the sound.

The Quiet Grace of Chaos

Like a drop of mercury in a veil of rain Azad catches the light. Like a firefly in Vegas he is unseen. Like a delta splits a river he confronts the tide—a lonely tree round which the ocean curls. Like a metaphor he is not what he seems. A lost monolith awaiting his calling, he walks through the streets of this synthetic valley.

A group passes now in cheap costumes, drama masks hiding their faces in their hoods. One boasts twisted horns, protruding bone from his forehead. Their chatter is full of laughter, drink and life. A massive explosion rings in his ears and Azad looks to the sky, lighting up in green and blue flowers, designs rotating and blooming on the bottoms of the clouds, now melting inward, until they are nothing again. Now for the lightworks, he thinks.

Liquid blue lights race up to the sky, to clouds tinted purple and rolling in the astral wind. Three birdwomen glide by beneath them, far above him, following the road to their destination. Their raincoats are shimmering and their wings are massive, feathered in gray, spanning a wide glistening arc through the remnants of the rain.

Beneath the dark blue and gray sky, a million green leaves on a hundred brown trees flicker, in the steadying wind, down the road, above the colorful raincoats, walking, riding in electric cars, above the slowly moving blades of grass. Buildings rise organically into the night—cylinders and hemispheres, spires, lights. Rails unfurl as spider-work, spanning the night with their web. A dark bird perches on a streetlight. Always the clouds are moving slowly over his head, shifting and dancing, improvising this song of the night.

He sees a wren nearby, poking it's head up from the grass. Azad watches as it flutters, landing in the road. One dark eye reflects an oncoming light. A taxi four thousand times its size is bearing down. The bird turns, toward him. Azad expects it to fly, but it does not, and the vehicle passes right over its head. It twitches, with a sudden flap of both wings rising to the night, riding on a strong wind, quickly gone in the thin curtains of the rain.

Our divisions are relative.

He laughs at himself. Billions of years given for you, bird. Every moment of sunlight and evolution, it ends and begins in you. Every spoonful of ocean is yours.

Know your worth.

Be free.

Coming to his home he holds a plastic bag in hand, marked with a chaos butterfly. Walking through the apartment he realizes its vacancy. Maybe she went to a party, he thinks, or to see Orion. Maybe she's feeling better. Azad hopes this is so, but the empty rooms do nothing to console his imagination. Orion's manifesto lights on the screen, drawing his attention.

On her bed he finds a red coat abandoned.

In the PT Rail Station he approaches a greeter-bot in a black top hat. "Hello, Azad," it says. "Happy New Year. Will you kiss me?"

Laughing, he queries the machine, "Where is my sister, Harmony?"

"She is currently in the industrial sector, moving from the SI complex to the Netherlands." It pauses for a second before it says, "Your train appears to be running late. Please hold. Now it has been rerouted. Now it is thirty seconds away. It will arrive at dock eleven."

After just a moment he asks, "Where is Orion?"

The bot looks at him, black hemispheres under its eyes. It says, "Orion was killed in an electrical accident during the Team Laser Assault, yesterday. We express our sympathy."

Azad blinks and says, "Thank you, machine."

"We express our sympathy," it repeats to his back as he walks away.

Eis Hegeisthai

Domes range into the Asturian hills, deserted of life. Paths cut over the ridges, clean and gray across the yellow and brown. A gliding robot, visible against the white of the mist, before the glow of the city, traces a clear horizon, climbing the long incline. The mountains are ancient, sculpted by the heave of time itself, old almost as the water, frozen now on the long blades of wintering grass. Flowers, large and wet with dark colors, creep in wild, broken patches amid the landscape.

Sayd sits beyond the crest of a plateau, on a gray block that is vented for airflow. It is connected by a trio of low, wide tubes to the silver domes of an underground factory, down the far hill.

He watches the snow falling on the wildflowers. Genex breeds, their seeds have escaped the city streets and are scattering on the wind through the countryside. A small bot lies a few feet away, torn open by two long, smoldering wounds. He is not entirely certain why he fired the dragon on it. It was just shredding the flowers.

For a moment in the light and snow he was alive. These things will not be undone. No matter my vengeance. No matter my punishment. There is no path from this.

Over the hill's rocky crown, the reflecting shimmer of Halcyon casts a rippled blue-silver crescent in the clouds. The AG spires reach high. A blast echoes from the city and he looks at the blue-gray sheet above the next high, distant mossy rise, as a barrage of artificial lightning bursts color the snow-flecked air.

Reflections scatter nearby on the steel and snow.

Now two veiled forms are rising over the hill's steep horizon. Walking through the foot-tall grass, Harmony is shrouded in black, watching her path. Day sees him as they come closer. He does not move. The falling snow quickens with their ascent, crystals growing to dime-size, moving carelessly from north to south, perpendicular to their direction. As she draws up nearer to him Harmony matches his eye with her own, distant green, and her skin beneath her hood is pale as the storm. "Harmony," he says.

"Sayd," she replies.

He says, softly, "I didn't expect you."

"Oh?"

"I love you."

"I know."

"It doesn't matter."

"No," she says weakly, unsure of what she is protesting. "You're bleeding." A rabbit moves across the grass.

"It's strange, Harmony."

"What do you mean?"

"How life is. Like a vapor." The white snowfall intensifies. "We're living in a dream." They wait. Sayd's hands are shaking. "Invisible. Like, it can't be seen. Like could you imagine ribs were invisible?"

Harmony and Day are silent. A wind comes, cold and fearsome. Then the snow lightens. Sayd says, "Love is like a vapor."

Looking him in the eye, she says now clearly, "I couldn't take losing you, Sayd. You left me. That's the truth. But I should have believed in you. I'll love you forever. You and Orion. Both."

"We've changed so much."

"No we haven't." She smiles with a sad, muted laugh. Sitting on the block with him, she remains a step away. She motions toward the SI, mostly hidden below them, with her hand, which hangs in the air. "Faith," her voice cracks on the name.

"The world has gone insane," he says quietly.

Day says weakly, "What are we supposed to do?"

In a toneless whisper he says, "Don't panic." She says nothing. He adds, "We should leave this place."

"How did that happen?" Harmony asks, shell-shocked.

He says, "My felon chip is malfunctioning." He hesitates. His eyes fall to where the bot is torn on the lawn. He pulls the laser from his coat pocket. Sayd does not raise his eyes, but says urgently, "This! I'm not moving my hand. The chip is on some runaway protocol. Fucking run." He throws the dragon with a sharp movement of his forearm. It slides into the snowy grass a few feet away. "Holy shit." He laughs, suddenly.

Harmony says, calmly, looking up at him, "I'm with you let's get out of here."

Day is the only one that moves, going to it without much hesitation. Bending down, she takes the weapon, looking at it, afraid as it shines with the fine, wet snow crystals, white on black.

With winter twilight on his shoulders Azad climbs the hill. Above him stand the rounded roofs of factories, pale horizons in the thickening fog of snow.

Visions of Orion are all around him. Every breath is a meditation on mortality. Each crystal flake is a reminder of the fleeting pointlessness of poetry. So he tries simply to breathe. But it does not come easily.

Yet there is release in death. There is peace in mystery, solace in emptiness.

There is grace in smallness, in the finite, eternal ending of each breath. Each blink of your eye will not come twice.

Orion spent so much time in words, in the mechanisms of life. So much pride in his creations. He wanted to recreate himself, in gears, in words to overcome mortality.

So it was with mankind.

An axiom, thinks Azad. The axiom is in me and this is what I know. I am the bridge. I am belief. I am a lens, of soul.

I, ambition.

Thinking on the manifesto, Azad continues, Yes, Orion. Energy pulses through electric circuits, but living minds may control it. Or maybe every stone has consciousness but not the hands to express it. A native response, instead of simulated. Life is more precious, something more than its moving parts.

How do I know? Knowledge is acceptance.

It is the first and the last thing I ever feel. It is my unique singularity and my common core. This intangible spark is the grail of awareness, the cosmic gap, creative light, immortal in itself and yet inextricably bound to flesh.

He smiles, thinking how people feared the momentum of years, the tsunami of the Ren, when it took their jobs. In the presence of the greatest treasures ever found they held on to silver coins. Were they just a vessel? After eons of suffering, labor, the new anti-economy looked them in the eye and said, Yes, it was all for nothing. Yes, your struggle is over and there will be no justice. Let it go. By mana, you are one soul with infinite eyes. Every crime you suffered, you committed. Let it go. Eternity smiles on you. At the doors of freedom men cowered, chained to their wealth.

Only when they gave it away did they finally own it.

That's no contradiction, he thinks, coming now to understand anew. It is consummation.

Privacy died, money vaporized. Yet the economics of production thrived as the future came to pass. Man, thinks Azad, even mankind herself came to change, in so many ways. New wings, same traps anyway.

Orion, my friend, what you have seen.

He thinks of a passage from a book:

Therefore give yourself to truth. Do not rush into the fire, yet do not unduly fear the end.

Death is but reunion.

Harmony speaks, "Where do we go from here?"

"Orion . . ." Sayd says only this.

Day has come a few steps nearer to them.

As he rises she moves back with the weapon, pulling it up with both hands. He strikes her once, quick with a palm to her chin, knocking her from her feet. She lets go of the dragon into the air, where he takes it up like a magnet in the snowfall. Day comes down on the stones. Grabbing his own wrist he pulls his arm in, backing up away from them both in the wet grass. "It's too late. Run," he says. "Get help."

Harmony stands, looking at him.

He swallows hard. "Help us!" he screams, pulling down on his other hand, unable to dislodge the weapon from his own fist. Looking up he speaks strangely, mixing languages, "Eis hegeisthai. Where you cannot follow."

Day slowly stands. Blood streaks through her blonde hair, trickling down her cheek. Her blue eyes are full of quiet, trembling fear.

Coming upon the plateau, Azad sees the three standing between the factory and the flowers. A cluster of Artisan bots moves toward them, still further off than he, approaching from the direction of the SI. Pushing on through the quickening snow he recognizes them all immediately. Harmony is on one side, Day is in the middle but further back, and Sayd is on the other. He has difficulty discerning the words until he is closer still. There is blood in Day's hair.

"Afto simantiko einai. Alitheia," Sayd is saying, trancelike, holding the black weapon with both hands.

Azad rushes to him, grabbing it, and Sayd looks at him with wide wild eyes. Though he does not fight for control, Sayd's grip tightens, and a ray ignites from the weapon. It vaporizes through Azad's coat.

It burns through Harmony's, through her skin and in through her chest all at once.

The wind rushes out of her. She lands on her knees. Harmony slowly gasps for air, drinking it, thick like water that pours right out.

She falls then to the earth.

Pebbles roll soft with soil at her step. Climbing the hill together under a broad sun, Azad looks at his sister's back, darker, the way the daylight falls into her, ascending toward blue sky.

Some of the trees are gnarled. As they pass there are insects that buzz away.

An explosion rings in the city, and the heavens are lit in gold. Fairies of light move across the bottoms of the clouds, and sparkling ashes fall in waves of color through the white night.

A blackbird passes between Harmony's eyes and the sky.

Azad kneels to her.

"Where have you been?" she asks.

Listening to the sounds, encroaching with the dusk, the vibrations and insect song, birds and the wilderness of the living, breathing earth, in the valley before the city came, Harmony and Azad hike up.

Leaves crumble beneath her feet.

A fresh wind rises steadily around them as she closes her eyes to the immediate pain. This sea of light. Her eyes crack open anyway. Tattered clouds are drifting slowly by, low through the snowstorm—gray, black on white.

Reality's final cry dies for Sayd as she falls. Pointing the dragon near Azad he pulls, but Azad does not flinch or turn.

Twin rivers streak his olive cheeks.

He thinks, There's no goodbye.

To his throat he points the weapon.

Azad looks up, shouting, "Don't!"

The dragon lights, and Sayd feels a sharp pain.

The atmosphere is riddled with ten thousand stars, shifting and flying, descending in glittering technicolor.

He hears Harmony, in a whisper, "I'm cold. I can't breathe. I can't . . . "

Azad's black hair is the wind, cresting the hill line.

Colors reflect in his iris, a wheeling prism. The black hole dilates. Father laughs. Yellow grass flares like the surface of the sun. Light is raining.

This moment passes quietly through him, and he is aware of many things—sharper than a word of pain, softer than a faded memory. Naked truth unwinds in his soul as words never quite spoken. I'm not happy, Azad. I'm unfinished and alone. My dreams are true and still I sleep. When I was young I knew it—not in the prison of words. My love. I'll remain in you. I will live forever.

You must see that love is the will—all paths.
Love is the mind—all thoughts.
Love is the body—all parts.
It is the only choice, of all or nothing.
It is the source. It is the well that never dries.
It is the ring and the ray—the satellite and the sun.
It is the one truth reflected in all things.

Know it. Own it.
Give it and be alive.

Rise in love.

Fly. In gravity.

She takes a breath, like a wind.

Day stands nearby, with her hands in the pockets of her raincoat. In her fist she grips a wet, wrinkled photograph. Wondering what it is she draws it out, and it is only a streaked blur of ruined gray. Whatever, she thinks. Nothing lasts. Help me. Oh fuck, help me please. Someone hold on to me. She drops the paper to the soaked earth. Her coat slips, down one arm to her elbow.

So Cry Out

In the factory hills outside of the valley Halcyon, a young girl stands. Releasing her raincoat from her arms it falls to the ground, curling in the wind, and she stretches her feathered wings. Azad kneels, leaning back with his sister, holding her. He looks, at length, to the stranger. Hesitating at the very edge of action, between reality and possibility, she appears a fragile creature.

Beyond the city of sapphire and diamonds, snow wanders down from crystalline heights. Spires glimmer on high, over the ridges and distance, the peaks of Halcyon, rising from the earth.

Blood runs in the grass, as truth fallen open at her sneakered feet.

In this symphony, the choir rests. A tenor line is mourning. Interwoven with their voices is a lonely, unheard string, the note of birth and death and dreams.

An Artisan carries off the body of Sayd. Limp in its long arms, he sways as it clambers over the rocks. One comes toward Harmony and a closer one moves toward Day. She retreats a step and it lowers, whirring, acting as though it is lifting something from the ground. On his knees, Azad pulls his sister away. The bot moves as if to lift her, cradling empty space. Bringing her hand to her chest Harmony cups blood, desperate and slow. As the Artisans move down the slope, the autodusters sterilize the ground where they were, and in front of where Day is standing.

A swath of ice ripples and falls from her wings.

Azad looks back to Harmony.

In his hands he feels the fragility of her breathing body, the warmth of the fire inside of her. Embers glow in the ashes of his broken heart, and the skyline flares. He is silent. He has no word adequate for this. It is the comet falling, scattered to glitter in the snow in the darkening sky, far like a silver butterfly—made of a thousand liquid crystals. The New Year's lightworks thunder, punctuating the silence of these hills.

Day steps forward, into the flowers.

Selected Poems
of
Joshua L Stelling

Silver Dawn

The sun grows heavy with my eyes
An apparition in the sky
A ghost of hope in days devoid
To you, great ball of burning fire
Goodbye

Tracing red and golden slivers
Cars wash by as if a river
Of electricity and rust
Of strange complacency and trust
To dust

As I bring fire from my fist
To the cigarette between my lips
Over asphalt lights flash on
As a prelude to the silver dawn

A slowly rising hemisphere
Of silver light, crisp and clear
A sentinel high in the void
The moon pierces the atmosphere
Aware

As I stare, come through the mist
Firelights of stars, distant, distinct
Rings of satellites turning
And galaxies of dust are whirling

Time is not a river, I think
But an ocean of oddity
Of this I am but one small drop
To you, sweet soothing silver rock
Goodnight

Angels

If you were going to read a poem
What would you want it to be?
Calm like a ray of light
An epic of destiny?
There is a light that glides
Across a wooden floor
A cosmic messenger
Translating stars
Through dust
Astronauts know
A new age has begun
It doesn't move, this light, but for the world
Spinning slowly
At my feet
A new age has begun
Though
There is darkness still in the wood
Its curves are like ribs
Curled into knots
Flat
Time was it was a tree
A nipple, a leaf
If you were going to live a life
What would you want it to be?
A passage through your time
A shifting of the sea?
Into the night it glides
The shuttle soars
A cosmic messenger
Rocketing us
Among the stars
The explosion will ring out for years
Angels in the sunlight, outside my window play
Their world has been turning
All this time

The Window

There is a glass wall in my prison
Through which the sunlight comes
Red and blonde
Blushing sky
Do anything you will to me
Torture me
Dehumanize
And I will have but one reply
Thank you for the window
I don't speak to my captors
They are not alive
They have no ears
They have no eyes
I speak only to the sky
I see only this window
Though my body is encaged
My love a parting dream
And the world a child's toy
I fly
With the bauble of the sun my soul will rise

Reaching In

I open my eyes and it is like the sun
This hand
Fingers rays
Reaching in like there's a hole in my chest
Light passes right through me
Or how do you explain my shadow?
We usually cannot see
The entirety of the line
Circles, we see blades of grass
This hand
Fingers rays
Touching upon my heart
Or how do you explain this warming?
There are things between
The two sides of a line
Infinity, we see blades of grass
I open my eyes and you are like the one
This girl
Eyeballs blaze
Coming in she burns a hole in the east
Her coat is open clouds
Or how do you explain the color?
We are so often blinded by
Things too large to understand
Idolatry, we're just blades of grass
This girl
Eyeballs blaze
Threading right back to the start
Across the sky she comes
This hand
Right through the veil she comes
Reaching into me
I watch, then blink
Waking with the sun

Promises

A covenant made between the seed and tree
Is a bridge that links
Activists and change
Godfathers and today
Baton and knee
Blood and stone
Youth and recklessness
Innocent to innocent
Toes and knee
Thigh and eye
Imagination and fortune
A vow kissed by the day
Never fades
We can walk like men on earth
Plow fields, give birth
Live in peace, cosmonauts
Love in peace, astronauts
Leaves bent, resilient
Bark strong, on a long limb
Give heifers to indigenous
People
The promise made by the leaf to the bird
Is a bridge
It carries the pain of distance
The confusion of home
Distraction of dreams
Abstraction
Of the palpable
Thick blood
The promise made by the wing to the day
Is that we are here

Silhouetted in the light
It's the word given by the preacher
To the lie
The politician to the grave
Scientist to anarchist
Child to policeman
Blood and stone
Innocent and innocent
Toes and knee
Thigh and eye
Bruised soul
A vow kissed by the day
Never fades
And we are here
So like the seed to the heavens
We are made and so will rise

Possessed

Sex is not a demon
Says the man with the horns
I look in his eyes and see
Mine
Your body is my temple
He says with my dick
In his hands
In the orgasm of
Celestial impertinence
We spiral out like galaxies
From the beginning to the end
Stretching our toes as if to express
Endlessness
To let out the feeling
Of a tongue on teeth
To breathe in you
Breathing in me
To give to you
What you give to me
Sex is not a whisper
But a drink of wine
You are internal
Eternally
Get into me
The beast is not a burden
From one to the next
We go on with our
Hate
Release me
Your body is my temple
Says the man with my stigmata
In his hands
I was born a cosmic child
I was born to give you love
I feel his hands and they are
Mine

No Abyss

Nightfall comes down
And the day does not forget
It fades
There is no abyss beyond the hill
Yet where I stand
Becomes darkness
What I saw
Turns to memory
The shivering leaves
Become shades
Ghosts embodied by the wind
Veins disappear
Your cheekbones become clear
Moreso in these shadows
Some things can be seen only in the darkness
Like the shimmering words
You spill
Curl like fairydust about the stars
Coming now down
As if there were no clouds
Some things cannot be seen in the darkness
Like the withering veins
Our age
It fades

Feathers

Submit to thc bcginnings of your life
As if the breakfast meal were a toast of wine
Words that echo days past
Come up through you
A bubble, a flower
That long thing, the shaft of time
Comes up through you
Babbling, River
We are a fall of water
Rush, and the persistence of gravity
Is long the same pull
Much as if time were a lover
In the beginnings of your life
Submit to the rhythm of my heart
As if the early toast were a daylong nap
With you laid upon me
Our whispers echoing eons past
And there was a crash of feathers

No Turn

Effortless as receiving a name
Is this whole search for character
There is no struggle or tragedy
Like a turn of a leaf in the wind
Decades of desk penance you condemn yourself to
Are nothing more than wage slavery
In the epic of the rains
Finding ourselves is no more intricate a path
Than taking off your clothes
How many leaves turning this way and that
Is something like all of the days that pass
And even when you forget your childhood
All of the life you wasted at that same desk
It still is a part of time

Two

The first thing you notice is how she enters a room
The break of light over mountains does it justice
The crash of color on countless bits of rain
The risen sun, the setting day, the start and the finish
one and the same
A crystal, fountainous with clouds and life
From the furthest crest of stones
To the perfect shades of overgrowth before you
There are the purrs, the engine and the curt, airy calls
of birds

Reckoning

Light as an arrow is the end of days
Like men singing who once held arms
Their melody is not without the pains of change
But a risen tide coming
Ravishing in the light